Sweet Temptation

Dara Girard

Sweet Temptation

Copyright © 2017 by Sade Odubiyi

ISBN 13: 978-1949764062

All rights reserved. No part of this publication may be reproduced, stored in a retrieval system, or transmitted in any form or by any means, electronic, mechanical, recording or otherwise, without the prior written permission of the Publisher, excepting brief quotes used in reviews.

Printed in the United States of America
Cover photo © 2017 pitrs/123rf
Cover and Layout Copyright © 2017 Ilori Press Books, LLC

This is a work of fiction. Names, characters, places, and incidents either are the product of the author's imagination or are used fictitiously, and any resemblance to actual persons, living or dead, business establishments, events or locales is entirely coincidental.

ILORI PRESS BOOKS, LLC
PO Box #10332
Silver Spring, MD 20914
www.iloripressbooks.com

Other Books by Dara

The Black Stockings Society
Power Play
A Gentleman's Offer
Body Chemistry
Round the Clock

Return of the Black Stockings Society
Playing for Keeps
After Hours
A Private Affair
Just One Look

Henson Series
Table for Two
Gaining Interest
Careless Rapture
Dangerous Curves
Familiar Stranger

The Clifton Sisters
The Sapphire Pendant
The Amber Stone

It Happened One Wedding
Unexpected Pleasure
Midnight Promise

Novels
Illusive Flame
Honest Betrayal
The Daughters of Winston Barnett
Remember My Name

Dear Reader,

Welcome to the third book in the *It Happened One Wedding* series where the best part of the story is after "I do."

Have you ever attended a wedding that didn't happen? Either the bride or groom didn't show, someone caused a disturbance or a secret was revealed?

I haven't (so far!), but I thought what if something awful happened that affected the lives of the family for years to come. That gave me the initial premise of the disaster that changed Clarice Yates life.

Strangely, her misfortunate, proved lucky for Drew Cutter and when their paths cross again temptation won't be the only feeling Clarice will try to resist.

I hope you enjoy *Sweet Temptation.*

All the best,

Dara

You can find out more about this series and learn about my other titles on my website www.daragirard.com

Chapter One

Speeding down a four lane highway with a crying four-year-old in the backseat and a screaming twenty-nine year old in the throes of labor beside her, didn't constitute a good day for Clarice Yates. Although the day itself had started off innocently enough. She'd even enjoyed a simple breakfast—melted Swiss cheese on toast with a glass of orange juice—which she rarely did because she was usually late for work after sleeping through her alarms.

She had three. One to wake her at six, which she immediately hit the snooze button. A second to wake her at six-thirty, this one she placed across the room on top of her dresser. She still managed to turn it off and crawl back into bed. The third she had in the hallway to go off at seven-fifteen, a noisy alarm that finally roused her. She'd once considered using it as her first alarm, but when she tried, it had so rattled her that she'd ended up smashing it with her fist while semi-conscious.

The three alarm system worked just enough to get her ready to head out the door while still not providing enough time for the barest of breakfast. She usually ended up getting a stale bagel and some cream cheese from a convenience store, a few blocks from downtown Temple Grove,

Maryland, where Yates Accounting Services, the business she ran with her mother, sat on the fifth floor of an eight level executive building. Temple Grove was experiencing a well deserved development boom, after being ignored for decades, sporting new apartments, retail stores and office buildings, which had made Yates Accounting Services extra popular with companies both large and small jockeying for space in the expertly designed township.

For Clarice, getting up on Mondays was harder than Fridays and she made special allowances for that.

But this Tuesday morning had been different. She didn't know why she'd woken up before the third alarm, but to her amazement she woke up semi-refreshed and alert enough to make breakfast and she also managed to enjoy sitting out on the patio (that she barely used) of her three level townhouse, listening to the sound of a robin singing while it sat on one of the bushes she needed to trim.

After working half the day, she'd left early and walked down the main street enjoying the spring weather, where only last week had been drenched by torrential rain. Today the sun decided to show its face, touching the budding blossoms on the dogwood trees that lined the parking lot. She had enjoyed her mini walk before picking up her sister and niece to go shopping to buy a gift, so her niece could attend a friend's birthday party.

It had all seemed so perfect. That should have warned her of what was to come.

"Don't cry, Maggie," Clarice said, trying to soothe her niece whose cocoa cheeks had a tinge of red.

"Her name is Marigold," her sister Faiza snapped.

"I'm not calling her that." Clarice softened her tone and addressed her niece again. "It's going to be okay, honey. Don't cry. Mommy will be okay."

Faiza gritted her teeth. "Mommy will not be okay if you don't do something."

"I am. I'm trying to get you to the hospital," Clarice said, trying her best to hide her exasperation. "I *told* you we should have waited for an ambulance."

"I thought we had time," Faiza shot back. "Marigold took six hours."

"Every pregnancy is different."

"I know that now!" she said, punctuating each word with an exclamation mark. "Can't you go faster?"

"I'm going as fast as I can. What do you expect me to do? Fly over traffic?" Although she wished she could. Traffic was heavy and there wasn't a cop in sight.

Faiza mumbled something then reached for her cell phone.

"What are you doing now?"

"Calling Carl." Her voice changed when her husband came on the line. "Yeah, baby hi. Um…I'm on the way to the hospital. Clarice's driving me. The baby's coming. I know. I know. I can't believe it either. I wanted you to be…Could you hold on a minute? I have to scream." Which she did long and loud, making her daughter cry even harder, before she picked up the phone again. "I know. It happened so fast I didn't get to call an ambulance. We'll soon be there. Yeah, that's Marigold…I know. I can't talk now…Love you too." She disconnected and tossed the phone on the seat before resting her hand on her stomach. "God, I wish he were here."

Clarice wished a lot of things. She wished she hadn't listened to her sister when Faiza complained of a little twinge when she noticed her sister wincing and rubbing her back when they were in the toy store. Nearby, a girl, who looked about seven, was bouncing a large green ball her mother couldn't get away from her. A few feet away from them another girl, glued to her cell phone, walked into a shopping cart someone had abandoned in the aisle, and a boy about six ran up and down the aisles chasing a teenage clerk who should have known better.

If she hadn't been so distracted trying to stop Maggie from talking at the top of her voice (she hadn't learned the benefits of an 'inside voice' yet) when she found something she liked, Clarice might not be in this situation now, but she hadn't paid attention to key signs. "He'll be there with you," Clarice said, trying to sound reassuring. Although part of her wanted to curse him. He was the reason for the last minute shopping spree because he'd forgotten to take Maggie last week, booking a photo shoot for one of his clients instead. Clarice had suggested that Faiza find something online, but her sister had preferred to get out of the house and go shopping.

Clarice glanced at her sister in the rearview mirror when she heard her moan. Faiza had her eyes closed, her head held back; one arm cupping her stomach. "You're doing great."

Her sister moaned again. Maggie continued to cry.

Clarice licked her lips and put the air conditioner on high, hoping the cold blast of air would help. She glanced at her sister once more and saw Faiza's eyes had opened and her position had shifted. She now had her arms by her sides, her hands gripping the seat cushion, her lips compressed as if she were bearing down.

Clarice's pulse quickened and her voice cracked in alarm. "You are not allowed to have this baby in the car."

Faiza briefly shut her eyes and said in a low voice of warning, "I won't if you get me to the hospital in time."

"I will. I just need ten minutes." She needed more time to include traffic lights, but she wanted to be optimistic.

"I don't think I have ten minutes."

"Try."

"I am, but this baby has a mind of its own."

"Breathe deep and cross your legs or something."

"Shut up and stop telling me what to do." She groaned.

"I thought you weren't due for another two weeks."

"Me too." She paused. "Everything had been perfect up un—" The remainder of her sentence became something unintelligible and was drowned out by Maggie's cries.

Clarice looked up and saw the sign for the hospital. "We're getting close. Maggie, dear, we're almost there! You'll get to meet your new baby sister soon."

"I think she's going to meet her now," Faiza said.

Clarice shook her head. "It's not like you to be pessimistic. I'm making good time."

"But my water just broke."

Clarice swore thinking of the grey cloth seats of the newly purchased white sedan. It would be hard to clean. She rubbed her forehead with trembling fingers, although the inside of the car was cold, beads of sweat gathered on her skin. "I can't believe this is happening to me."

Faiza's voice rose in outrage. "To you! What about me? Do you think I planned it this way?" Tears entered her voice. "Carl was supposed to be here with me. It's not like you to be selfish."

"I'm not being selfish. I'm upset because this isn't my car."

"Whose car is it?"

"Mom's."

It was Faiza's turn to swear. "Why do you have Mom's car?"

"Because mine's in the shop and I told her I just needed it for a few errands." Clarice glanced at the clock. "I'm supposed to pick her up at the office in an hour." She hadn't told her mother that she was seeing her sister today. Her mother and Faiza had been estranged for years.

"Well you can't."

"Thanks for stating the obvious, but now that you know, you realize that I have to be extra careful with her prized possession. I can't be both late *and* ruin her car."

"Pull over."

"Just let me get past this green light."

"I said pull over. Now."

Clarice looked around, but she was effectively boxed in from the left to the right; front and back. "Give me a minute."

"Fine."

She heard her sister go quiet then looked at her in the rearview mirror and saw her taking off her panties. "W-what are you doing?"

"Getting ready to have a baby," she said calmly.

"I told you, you can't have the baby in here. What will I tell Mom?"

"I don't care."

"You never do," Clarice grumbled.

"That's not fair. I…" She swore then let out a low hiss. "Pull over dammit!"

Clarice managed to pull out from the cars and sped up.

"What are you doing?" her sister demanded. "I told you to pull over."

"I'm trying. I have to find enough space. The cars are speeding down fast."

"Clarice, I know you like to follow the rules. But I need you to do something reckless. Illegal if you have to. This is happening fast and I'm scared. I need you to—"

"I know. I know, all right." Clarice looked at her rear and side mirrors. She was going to have to take a chance. "Hold on," she said then quickly swerved to the shoulder of the road amid the honking of horns and the blast of a large truck whose horn sounded like a swear word.

She pulled over far enough on the shoulder to safely get out of the car as traffic continued to whiz past, the wind striking her skin like sheets of waves. *Just hold on. Just hold on. We're almost there,* she silently pleaded, hoping to get her sister out of the car and onto the grass. She hurried to the other side of the car and opened the back car door. "I really think I should—"

But the words died on her lips when she realized her sister wouldn't make it out of the car and neither would her new niece. Within moments her mother's car interior was ruined and a new life entered the world, with Clarice moving fast enough to catch her.

Soon the baby's loud cry mingled with the sounds of that of her older sister, and then Faiza started crying as well.

"Oh my God," Faiza said.

Clarice rested the baby in her sister's arms. She had taken off her jacket and used it to swaddle the baby to keep it warm. "You did it."

"Yes, I know. She's so tiny. With how big I was you would have thought she would have been larger."

"She looks perfect to me."

Faiza couldn't stop a smile. "Of course."

Clarice looked at Maggie and lightly touched her tear stained face. Her cries had reduced to hiccups. "See your new sister?" She straightened and got into the driver's seat again. "Now I have to get you two to the hospital." She started the ignition.

Faiza took a sharp intake of breath. "Oh no."

Clarice stopped before merging into traffic. "What?"

Her sister's face changed. "I feel like I have to push again."

"It's probably the afterbirth," Clarice said, quickly shutting off the engine. She jumped out and rushed to her sister's side, holding out her hand. "Quick, get out of the car before you—"

But once again, Clarice wasn't allowed to finish as another baby made its appearance. She stared at her sister startled. "You didn't tell me you were carrying twins."

"I didn't know. Do you think I would have kept this a secret? Oh my God this is crazy!"

Clarice looked down at the baby who was even smaller than its twin. "It's a boy."

"Well, this explains a lot. No wonder I looked like I was eating for three."

Clarice rolled her eyes. "You weren't that big."

Another car stopped and a couple came to help, the man mentioning he was a nurse. He helped Faiza through the remainder of the birth, cutting the umbilical cord and handling the afterbirth. Clarice then cleaned up as best she could using water from a bottle she always had with her, before she and his companion wrapped both babies in a blanket her mother kept in the trunk in case of emergencies. As she drove to the hospital Clarice searched her mind for the best lie to tell her.

Chapter Two

The hospital bustled with an array of sounds—people rushing through the white tiled corridors, the sound of a trolley racing down the hallway. Clarice knew she couldn't give her mother a clue as to where she was, so she decided to make a call outside in the back entrance far from the emergency department. A place that smelled like old cigarettes and asphalt.

"Where are you?" her mother demanded the moment she picked up.

"Sorry, something came up. But a car will be there to give you a lift shortly."

"Why can't you pick me up?"

"I'll explain later."

"You'll explain now. Are those sirens I hear?"

"Just one passing down the street."

"They sound awfully close. Oh no. Did you get into an accident? Did something happen to my car?"

No and yes. "Relax, Mom everything will be fine."

"Clarice, what have you done?"

"Sorry what?" Clarice said, pretending not to hear her. "What was that?" She paused between her words to mimic interference. "Oh…no… think…connection…bad."

Her mother raised her voice. "Clarice, I—"

"Nope. Can't hear a word. Sorry Mom. Talk to you soon. Bye." She disconnected. The cell phone rang again with loud urgency. She turned it off. Her mother would read her the riot act later, but right now she wanted to see if her sister was okay.

Clarice turned to go inside then froze when she saw a familiar face from her past exiting through the wide glass doors. Luisa Morales was one of her former teachers at the massage school she'd attended years ago. Clarice stood still and barely breathed, as if that action would make her invisible. She didn't want her former teacher to see her and ask the inevitable questions like "How are you?" "What are you doing?" "Did you ever open your own business?"

Clarice held her breath as Luisa passed her, amazed that she hadn't been noticed. Perhaps her luck had changed. She released a breath when Luisa stepped off the pavement and headed for the parking lot.

That's right. Keep walking. Keep walking.

Clarice gripped the phone in her hand. *Yes, she was going to be safe. Victory!* But her breath caught when Luisa suddenly stopped.

Please don't turn around. Please. Please. Please.

Luisa turned in her exquisitely designed black shoes and her face spread into a wide smile. "Clarice Yates?" She held out her arms wide. "I thought it was you!"

Clarice plastered on a smile and stared at the attractive woman whose once dark hair was now a honey brown, and her deep red lipstick would have made a less vibrant woman of a certain age look trashy, but only made her more alluring. "Ms—"

Luisa embraced her before she could speak, enveloping her in the scent of warm ginger and coconut.

Clarice awkwardly embraced her back. "Yes. It's me. This is a surprise."

"Yes, I work here now. But enough about me. I want to know all about you."

"There's not much to say."

Luisa's expression dimmed with sympathy. "How is your mother?"

"I'm working with her. Business is booming."

Her bright smile returned. "So you did it?" she said, clasping her hands together. "You opened your own clinic? I knew you would. That was your dream."

"No," Clarice said, sorry to disappoint her. "I'm still working with my mother in accounting."

Her expression dimmed again, like a cloud covering the sun. "Oh."

"But I still renew my license. I don't know why."

"Because it's what you love." She sighed. "What you're meant to do." She tilted her head then pointed at her. "I might have a job for you. It's not many hours, but the money is good. I'd need you to take a skills test, but if you pass, at least you could help me with some of my senior patients."

Clarice felt her heart racing. Could this really be happening? Could she really get the chance to finally use her massage skills? A second chance? "Okay."

"I'm taking interviews next month." She scribbled something on a business card before handing it to her. "Come to this address at ten on the date I put on the back. I look forward to seeing you." She winked then left.

Clarice held the card to her chest and closed her eyes. She wanted the chance to get into the massage therapy field so much she could feel it, but she wasn't sure she could—or should—take the chance. She hadn't told Luisa that she would show up.

She tucked the card away. No one in her family knew about her secret passion. A passion that had slowly built when she'd broken her arm and damaged her shoulder after crashing her bicycle at twelve years old. She'd received physical therapy and a new fascination had been ignited. She didn't want to be a doctor or a nurse. She liked the language of massage, the atmosphere, the energy. In college she'd taken the requisite courses to become a public accountant, but on the side she'd taken other courses, including the ones with Luisa, that met her interest. Neither her mother nor sister took much notice.

So she'd never shared that she'd passed the massage and bodywork licensing examination. That Luisa had asked her to work with her. And she still wasn't sure she was ready to tell anyone that. She'd think about Luisa's offer, but doubted she'd accept. She'd chosen her path and didn't think anything could change that. Not without causing pain. And her family had experienced enough of that already.

Moments later, Clarice walked into the cream colored hospital room and greeted her brother-in-law, Carl Siggins, who was holding Maggie. Her niece was now all smiles as she rested her head on her father's shoulder. "To the woman who saved the day," he said when Clarice entered the room.

Clarice held up her hands fending off his praise. "I didn't do anything. And the day hasn't ended yet," she said in a grim tone.

Faiza winced in sympathy as she held the two sleeping infants in her arms. Without her features twisting in pain she was a sight to behold with smooth mahogany skin and well-modeled, delicate features. "Did you talk to her?"

Clarice nodded, knowing who she meant. Although she hadn't done as much work as her sister had, she felt exhausted and knew it probably showed on her face. Her features were far from delicate and dark chocolate freckles spread over her pecan colored skin and always seemed more evident when she was stressed. She imagined she could easily imitate a chocolate chip cookie right now.

"How was she?"

Clarice walked over to the bed, seeing the worry in her sister's eyes. "Ready to take my head off, but I can handle that," she said, forcing a laugh that made her sister look more at ease. "How are you?"

"Still in shock." Faiza glanced at her husband amazed. "We didn't prepare for this."

Carl lifted the camera he had hanging around his neck, instantly changing into the photographer he was. He was a man of average height who carried himself as if he were taller, with broad shoulders and a smile that got him as much referrals as his work did. "Let me take a picture."

"Don't you dare!" Faiza said. "No pictures. My hair isn't done and I look a mess."

He kissed her forehead. "You always look good to me," he said then took the photo.

"Beast," she said with affection. "Give me another kiss."

He obliged.

Clarice sighed, eager to leave. As much as she was glad to see them happy in the throes of marital bliss their show of affection still made her feel uncomfortable. "I guess I'll get going."

"No, stay a little longer," Faiza said. "Dad will be here soon."

Carl nodded towards Maggie. "And I was going to treat this little one to something sweet. Why don't you join us?"

"Sorry, I can't. Talk to you later." She turned to the door.

"Clarice wait."

She slowly turned back sensing the urgency in her sister's voice and steeling herself against it. "What?" she said determined to keep a light tone.

Faiza's brown gaze turned serious. "You don't have to lie. You can tell her the truth. About us. About what happened. About everything."

Clarice bit her lip, a flicker of hope entering her heart. Could she do that? Could she tell her mother the truth? She glanced at Carl for support, but he lowered his gaze, leaving her feeling alone. It was a feeling she'd grown used to. She took a deep breath and shook her head. "The truth will hurt more. I'm not ready to do that."

"We can't lie to her forever."

"Maybe you can't," Clarice said, turning to the door. "But I've made it a habit."

Forever was a long time. Clarice knew she could lie to her mother, but avoiding her was getting difficult. She'd managed to skip work for a day and had ignored her calls. She'd left a message that she needed the car a little longer, but at the office the following day, her mother marched into her office determined to get answers. At barely five foot two, Lois Yates was used to getting them. Today she wore a dark pant suit with a purple blouse, her hair coiffed to perfection. She pounded her fist on the desk. "I don't see my car in the regular space. What happened to it?"

"I had to take it to get cleaned," Clarice said, knowing it was best to remain calm. Lying while excited or distressed never went over well.

Lois folded her arms and glared at her. "You did get into an accident, didn't you?"

"No," Clarice said in the same calm voice. "It was nothing like that."

"I let you borrow my beloved baby for one day." She waved her finger. "One day! And you get it into an accident?"

Clarice gritted her teeth and counted to ten. *Calm. Remain calm.* "I told you it wasn't an accident. I gave a friend a lift and her little girl got sick in the back. I couldn't clean it all up."

"You could have worn a mask and saved money."

Clarice made a face. "It was a lot and it smelled bad."

Lois curled her lip in distaste. "This is still an inconvenience."

"It will be ready by tomorrow," Clarice said with a smile that her mother trusted.

"It better be," she said before she left.

Clarice let out a sigh of relief. Lying to her mother had become routine but no less difficult. Part of her wanted to tell her mother that she was now the grandmother of twins as well as a niece who would soon turn five. That Faiza's vintage shop was doing well and so was Carl's business, but what would have been good news to others would only be poison to Lois and Clarice knew news like that would only hurt her.

But it still didn't stop Clarice from wanting to share the wild adventure she'd had with Faiza on the side of the road, but she had to keep that to herself as well. As she had to do most things: Like the fact that she was bored of her job—of her life really—and longed for more. But her mother's life had become so insular that Clarice was one of the few people she had left. She'd been hurt and Clarice couldn't abandon her. She'd been her mother's lifeline since the wedding that changed all their lives.

Chapter Three

Eight years ago

A declaration of love is always a beautiful sight at a wedding. Unless it comes from someone other than the bride and groom.

"I love you!" Faiza called out as she stood among the hundred of guests and shouted her feelings to the groom who stood by her mother's side. A collective gasp filled the church pews.

Someone sitting beside her tugged on her arm and tried to pull her down, but she wouldn't move. "Please, don't do this."

Clarice stood by her mother's side wearing a strapless lavender bridesmaid's dress and cleared her throat. She turned to the pastor who looked like a startled fox, his skin as red as his hair and his blue eyes wide. "I apologize," Clarice said. "My sister probably hasn't recovered from a night of partying, just ignore her."

"I can't." These words weren't spoken by the pastor but by the groom. Carl looked down at his bride with regret. "I'm sorry."

"You can't do this to me," Lois begged, her tiny hand gripping his sleeve. "Don't shame me like this in front of all of these people."

"I'm sorry," he said again then turned and met Faiza in the middle of the aisle. Together they dashed out of the church. Clarice stared at them open mouthed.

Her mother screamed.

The guests looked at each other in confusion, sounds of shock and amazement now filling the once quiet church.

Clarice tried to calm her mother, but she collapsed in her arms, leaving Clarice to take care of the aftermath. She had to cancel the reception, return the gifts and try to settle all the bills.

Three weeks after the wedding debacle—after her sister sent Clarice a picture of herself and her new husband on their honeymoon in Las Vegas where they'd eloped; after Clarice had had to rouse her mother out of bed to get showered at least once every few days. After she'd fielded questions from family and friends about how her mother was doing (terrible)—she received a knock on her office door at Yates Accounting Services and her office manager, Bob Mueller, opened the door to a young man dressed in jeans and a chef's jacket who stormed in holding a piece of paper and a large envelope.

Although he looked fierce the effect was lessened by the fact that he looked as if he'd just come out of culinary school and his voice had cracked yesterday. Tall and lanky, he had some fuzz above his top lip, which seemed like an attempt to look older, but failed, and skin the color of maple syrup.

"Sorry to barge in like this but it's been three weeks and I've sent the invoice three times."

Clarice paused. Whoa the kid's voice was deep. He may have looked like he'd just come out of high school, but he had the voice of a man. She frowned. "Invoice?"

He nodded and took a seat. "For the wedding."

Clarice felt her blood go cold. There was someone she'd forgotten to pay? She prided herself on being organized. She was an accountant for goodness' sakes. How could she have an outstanding balance?

She turned to her computer. "What's your name again?"

"Drew Cutter."

Clarice couldn't stop a smile. "I mean the name of your company."

"Oh, Delites."

She found their account and swore. When she looked through the list of items she swore some more. She'd tried to curb her mother's spending on the wedding, but she hadn't succeeded. Her mother had bought the best. She chewed her lip. "This can't be right."

"It is. Everything was delivered and we even have photos as proof." He set a thick manila envelope on the table.

"I believe you," she said, ignoring it. "Ratatouille costs this much?"

The young man opened the envelope then held out a picture to her. "It's not just ratatouille. It was one of the main entrees. A garden ratatouille served on buttered fettuccine with grated parmesan."

She nodded, absently licking her lip at the description, her eyes skimming over the line item for the basil crusted halibut and garlic whipped twice baked potato. She inwardly moaned that she'd missed the chance to eat them. "It sounds delicious, but did it really cost this much?"

"Yes, we made everything clear up front. I also have the contract in case—"

"I don't need it," she said, waving him away, but he still placed that on the table as well. "I see half has already been paid."

He nodded. "Yes."

"Could I talk to the owner?"

"I am the owner."

She met his eyes. *Yeah, right kid and I own a mansion in Georgia.* "Really?"

"Yep."

She wasn't in the mood to call his bluff. It was already embarrassing that she had to deal with this kid to handle her mother's awful wedding debacle. "Can we come up with a payment plan?"

"No, the agreement was for two payments."

Clarice drummed her fingers on the desk, studying him. He wouldn't be easy to manipulate although he was young. He had the look of someone who'd come for his money and didn't plan to leave until he got it. She couldn't blame him and admired him a little for it. She'd been in the position where she'd given people the benefit of the doubt and been disappointed. But that didn't make things easier for her or less painful.

She'd thought she'd put that miserable day behind her and now he was reminding her of it and how much it had cost them financially. Every line item was a betrayal, a broken promise, a shattered heart. She wanted to be angry at someone and Drew Cutter was an easy target.

She wrote down a number and pointed to it. "I'll pay you this amount or you can see me in court."

A vulnerable look entered his gaze. She kept her expression composed, not letting her eyes leave his face. *Yes, little boy I've been in business longer and have dealt with more people. If you want to leave empty handed today, that would be your choice.*

He blinked. "But—"

"But what? Should I write this check or not?"

He spread out the pictures across the table. "You see this? This is what you paid for. The finest around."

She fought hard not to look at the pictures. "I don't care."

Anger lit his brown gaze. "You should care." He pointed to the wedding cake. "That alone was worth the price of everything."

Clarice lifted the photograph up and studied it. The cake looked gorgeous. The detail immaculate. If she could have licked the photo she would have. A three tiered masterpiece with lemon cake and blackberry jam on one tier, green tea cake with white chocolate filling on another and strawberry cake on the last tier, the outside decorated with pink ombre buttercream icing and sugar flowers.

She set the picture down and pushed it away. "Impressive, but I haven't changed my mind."

He snatched the contract. "Fine. Then I'll see you in court."

She nodded. "Very well."

He stormed out and slammed the door.

Clarice sighed, she'd hoped he would have taken the money. Her offer had only shaved off a small percentage of the bill. But on the other hand, by him leaving it would give her time to strategize how she would be able to cover the entire cost. Perhaps she could get her sister to help some. Unfortunately, Faiza had complained that all her money had gone into moving her things into Carl's place and Carl's financial contribution had been minimal since her mother had wanted to stage her dream wedding no matter the cost.

Her sister and Carl were already living their happily ever after while Clarice and her mother were picking up the pieces.

She looked at some of the photos still spread out on her desk—the food looked so good, she could just imagine twirling the fettuccine on her fork the scent of butter and parmesan floating up to her as she stabbed the ratatouille and raised it to her lips… She turned the pictures over and swallowed back tears. No use looking back. No use thinking what might have been.

A few minutes later she heard a knock on the door. "Come in."

Bob peeked his head in with a look of sympathy. "There's someone here to see you—again."

"Fine. Let him in," Clarice said, guessing who the visitor would be.

Drew entered the room looking a little chagrined, but not enough to make her feel sorry for him. "Let's start again," he said, his deep voice still surprising her and stirring her senses. She found it a little unsettling how much she liked it. *You're a grown woman of twenty-six for goodness' sakes. Snap out of it!* He held out his hand. "I'm Drew Cutter with Delites."

She shook his hand—large, firm, warm—and motioned to a seat, which he took. "And you're here to settle your bill," she said ready to play along. "I apologize for the delay. Did your father tell you to come back and accept my offer?"

She saw his jaw twitch and hid a grin when he said, "*I* decided that it was best we settle the matter here," he said.

"Yes, would you like anything to drink? Coffee? Tea?"

"Tea, but only if it's real."

She paused. "What's unreal tea?"

"That herbal stuff. You might as well just squeeze water from a sponge."

Clearly not a fan of herbal teas then. She lifted a brow. "A tea aficionado?"

"No, British parents. I've learned not to touch the other stuff."

"Hmm, but I love wild raspberry. And chamomile is so soothing."

He tapped his chest. "I'm a black tea man through and through."

Clarice grinned. "Obviously."

He hesitated, clearly confused by her expression. "No, I mean. I like black tea not that I'm a black man." He paused. "Although I am a black man." He shook his head. "Never mind."

Clarice bit her lower lip to keep from laughing. "We might have jasmine tea, but that's it. I'm sorry to disappoint you," she said making a mental tally of the sparse collection they had in their break room.

"Never mind. I'm fine."

She took out a pen. "Are we in agreement then?"

He rubbed his chin. "Just add a hundred."

"No."

He ducked his head looking both fierce and vulnerable at the same time, in a way she'd never seen before. "Seventy-five?"

She shook her head then pointed at him. "You really need to work on your poker face. I can read every emotion there."

"Twenty-five is my final offer," he said.

Clarice started to put her pen away. "Okay."

He waved his hands. "Okay, okay. Fine you win," he said with all the enthusiasm of a child who'd lost his toy.

"Good." She wrote the check then handed it to him. "Thank you."

He stood and took the check. "You're welcome." He turned, walked to the door then looked down at the check and halted. He spun around and stared at her. "Wait, you gave me the entire amount."

"Yes, I did."

He blinked quickly. "B-but you said you wouldn't."

She nodded. "Yes, I did."

He sat down. "B-but you gave me such a hard time. Why did you do that if you were going to give me the money anyway?"

"Because I was mad at you. Not because you did any- thing wrong," she said quickly when he opened his mouth to argue, "but because I've been having a bad day. A bad couple of days. Weeks even, and you were an easy target." She pointed to the check with her pen. "Now we're even. Is there something else?" she asked when he hesitated, opening and closing one hand in his lap.

"Would you like to go out some time?"

Clarice had to bite her lip to keep from laughing. Was this kid serious?

Although she didn't laugh out loud, her amusement hurt him and showed in his eyes. He stood. "Never mind."

"Oh, so I don't even get a chance to consider it?"

His eyes lit with hope. "Would you?"

"Not with someone so quick to take the offer away."

He looked unsure and she knew she was being unfair to tease him, but couldn't help herself. He frowned. "You're messing with me again, aren't you?"

"No," she said and this time she was sincere. "I may have said 'Yes I'd love to go out with you' and force you to cook me something on this menu with the perfect wine pairing. Are you old enough to drink?"

He flexed his hand again and nodded. "So is that a yes?"

"I said 'may have'. Unfortunately, you said 'never mind' before I could answer so now it's neither here nor there. Bye, Mr. Cutter."

He scratched the side of his forehead, tucked the check away in his pocket then folded his arms. "Give me another chance."

"If I weren't already seeing someone, I would." She wasn't seeing anyone, but he didn't need to know that.

"Really?"

"Yes, besides I'm a lot older than you."

He lifted his chin. "I'm older than I look."

She couldn't stop a smile. "No you're not."

His hands fell to his hips. "How old do you think I am?"

"If you told me you were more than twenty-two I'd be shocked."

He looked surprised then disappointed.

"But it doesn't matter," she continued, "because the right woman won't care how old you are."

He nodded then started to turn and stopped. "If you want anything from that menu just let me know."

"Yes, I have your number. And I know how much it will cost."

"I'll give you a discount."

She smiled at him. "I'll remember that."

He hesitated as if he wanted to say something else then gave a little wave before he left. She was a little sorry to see him go because he was the only bright spot in a very bleak month. She'd been flattered by his attention, although it was strange and misplaced. Did he think he could have gotten her to pay more if he charmed her?

Whatever his reasons he was now gone. She'd paid in full knowing she'd figure out how to replenish her savings another time. Right now she had to deal with the reality of her broken family. It was only several days ago when she'd finally heard her mother's voice again.

"I'll never speak to her again," her mother had said after weeks of staying in bed and not talking or seeing anyone. Clarice had been clearing the untouched tray of food from the bed when her mother finally spoke in an angry whisper.

"I won't. Ever. I'll never speak to her. Or him. Or anyone. Did you know about them?"

Clarice set the tray on the ground and sat down on the side of the bed. "Of course not, Faiza said their feelings were unexpected but Carl never cheated on you."

"She still stole him."

Clarice tried to keep her voice gentle, knowing her words may hurt. "Mom, Carl did tell you he had doubts."

"Typical cold feet," Lois said. "He would have gotten over them."

"But he said it more than once. And I even tried to say—"

"It was my special day," her mother said, ignoring her. "It would have been perfect."

"That I didn't feel it was right between the two of you and that you may be pressuring him into something he didn't want."

"We would have been perfect." Lois smoothed down her short tightly curled hair. "People are always surprised when I tell them my age."

"But you didn't listen."

"I'd planned everything to the finest detail and I loved him."

Clarice sighed, defeated. "Just as you're not listening to me right now."

"But your sister ruined it."

She covered her mother's cold hand. "Mom, you need to eat something. I know you're upset—"

"Upset? They humiliated me in front of everyone. I'm more than upset. I'm mortified! How can I face people again?"

"You did nothing wrong. Hold your head high." Clarice stood and lifted the tray. "Let me reheat this so—"

"Don't bother. I won't eat it and don't tell me that I have to. My daughter ran off with my fiancé. I will never trust anyone again," she said, burying herself under the covers again.

And she didn't. She let friendships fall away. Kept her distance from family until Clarice was all she had left and to fill the time when she wasn't with her daughter, Lois filled it with her work.

And she had plenty of it. They now had so much of it they turned clients away. The Yates Accounting Services became even more successful after the debacle happened than it had been before. Clarice poured everything into the business and helped her mother establish something to be proud of. She was proud to help her create something to help her forget the pain of the past.

And in the ensuing years, Clarice had to pretend that she didn't have a sister. Her mother wouldn't mention Faiza's name (or Carl's) and visibly withered or became angry any time Clarice mentioned her sister, even in passing. So they lived with a ghost between them. Her father helped to make it bearable for her, being the one person who understood Clarice's conflict and someone she could turn to.

Faiza tried many times, in the first few years, to reach her mother—through notes, gifts, phone calls, emails, but her mother wouldn't budge. The notes were burned, the emails deleted, the gifts donated or returned; the phone calls erased.

Eight years Clarice had to pretend she lived two lives. Her mother knew she had contact with her sister, but as long as Clarice didn't say anything, she didn't feel betrayed.

Nothing would ever be the same. Faiza and Carl became parents.

Her mother became a recluse.

And Clarice lived in the nowhere space between them.

Chapter Four

Present Day

The weekend party seemed better suited for a debutant ball than a five-year-old's birthday. The grand rental hall and luxurious decorations were lost on the group of children being entertained by a clown, balloon animals, and face paintings. But what took center stage was the cake, an incredible delight that stood as tall as the birthday girl, decorated in the style of a castle.

Clarice helped a group of three little ones go to the bathroom when she noticed a young boy with short cropped black hair, bright blue sneakers and skin the color of pine nuts who seemed about seven or eight standing in front of a utility closet looking anxious. He briefly caught her eye and opened his mouth then closed it, as if he wanted to say something to her but was afraid to. She returned the kids to the party then returned to the hall surprised to still see him there. Perhaps he was supposed to chaperon his younger sibling and had lost track of him or her. She walked over to him.

"Is something wrong?" she asked him.

He rubbed his hands together and bit his lip. "I'm not supposed to say anything."

"Why not?"

He briefly turned towards the utility closet. "Because he'll get mad."

"Who?"

He bit his lip again. "Are you a doctor?"

"Do you need a doctor?"

He shifted from one foot to the other then stared at the ground.

"If you need help you can trust me," she said, making sure to keep her voice gentle. He looked very distressed and she didn't want to frighten him. "If someone is hurt they need help."

He chewed his lip then sighed. "Can you keep a secret?"

"Depends on the secret. But that's not the point. Is there something going on behind those doors that I should know about?"

"I was supposed to keep watch, but…" He sighed again, mumbled something under his breath then said, "Come on."

Clarice followed him into the closet her mind trying to imagine what she would find.

Nothing matched what she did see: A man, naked from the waist up, lying on the floor twisted in agony. She raced over to him and dropped down to her knees beside him, her floral print flare skirt billowing around her like a mushroom. She looked up at the young boy stunned. "This is what you're keeping a secret? Why would you do that?"

The boy continued rubbing his hands looking unsure. "He told me not to tell anyone."

Clarice returned her gaze to the man in front of her. His eyes were closed and sweat glistened on his brown skin. "Sir, don't worry. I will call an ambulance."

"No, ambulance," he said through gritted teeth.

"But—"

Angry brown eyes met hers. "I said no ambulance."

She looked at the boy hoping for more sanity than the man could give her. "What happened?"

"He slipped and fell," the boy said. "Luckily, it was after we'd delivered the cake or that would have been bad. But it was when he was going to get something from the truck that he slipped on the grass or something and he went down hard. I mean really hard. I wanted to get help, but he said not to and he seemed okay for a while but then came in here because—"

"Theo," the man said in a cutting tone effectively shutting the young boy up. He took a deep breath that made his entire body shudder. "I'll be fine."

"No, you won't," Clarice said, trying her best to assess the situation.

"It's a back spasm. Usually I have a friend who helps me, but I'll…just have to wait it out."

Theo folded his arms. "Yes, she gives him a message."

"Massage?" Clarice clarified.

He nodded. "I helped take off his shirt and he told me what to do, but I was only hurting him," he said in regret.

Clarice knew what she could do, but wasn't sure. "You really should see a doctor, but I think I can help."

The man stared at her, hope mingling with the pain in his gaze. "You know massage?"

"Yes, I studied." *Graduated top of my class although I haven't used it since.*

She looked around and took a ball down from one of the shelves and placed it under his knees, causing him to release a deep, aching groan. She searched her memory for the best strategy. She didn't have the benefit of a mattress, oils, or the right environment, but if she could loosen the spasm then he wouldn't be in so much pain. "This is not ideal, but I'll do my best. So try to relax and trust me."

She knew that wouldn't be easy, but she was all he had at the moment. Fortunately, he was as well made as the anatomy doll she'd practiced on. He was pure sleek muscle, his skin tight against his form, making it easy for her to know every oblique, dorsal and subclavial muscle. And he smelled like vanilla extract and sweetened almonds.

He grimaced when she lightly probed the muscles in his shoulder and upper back, gently working her way in and out over the entire width of his back. But although she was barely applying friction the pain on his face hadn't shifted. She didn't think it was wise to go deeper.

"Ready to give up?" he whispered.

She wasn't sure if that was a challenge or a resignation, but it stirred a new fire within her. She didn't plan to fail him or herself. "Open your eyes and focus on something."

"Why?"

"Because you need to distract yourself from the pain."

He opened his eyes and studied her, his jaw tight as if he was waiting for the moment she'd hit a nerve and send him into renewed agony. Her face burned under the scrutiny and she could imagine him inspecting her freckles, but she didn't want to lose sight of her purpose. He could stare at her all he wanted as long as she succeeded in her task— giving him relief. The seconds seemed to tick away at a glacial pace, but she steadily kept probing his muscles until they eased under her insistent pressure.

Soon his tight muscles became supple under her hand. She heard and felt him sigh. Slowly the hard jaw softened and his eyes closed, this time not from pain but from relief.

"Did you fall on your back?" she asked.

"No, my hip."

It seemed strange to her that the entire length of his back seemed to bother him rather than an isolated spot. He winced when he shifted position so she continued kneading his back in long smooth strokes.

"Grandma thinks he has sky gottic ya," Theo said.

"What?"

"Sciatica," the man clarified.

"Oh. It doesn't seem to be that, but a doctor may be able to make a diagnosis."

They fell quiet again and she continued her rhythmic motion. She then rested her hands flat on his back signaling she was done.

"Better?"

"Hmm."

"That means yes," Theo said.

She smiled at the young boy. "Thank you, but I still think he needs a longer soft tissue massage, but I'm not sure that will do much in the long term." She watched the man as he slowly sat upright. "Perhaps if you saw a specialist like a rheumatologist they could help you."

"Maybe," he said sounding doubtful. He put on his black T-shirt. "How much do you charge?"

"Charge?"

"For massage."

Clarice rose to her feet and wiped her hands together. "Oh…I'm not a professional."

"You acted like you knew what you were doing," he said in a voice that was so beautifully deep it caused goose-bumps to form along her arms.

Clarice cleared her throat suddenly feeling both hot and cold at the same time, wondering what was affecting her more. His sharp brown eyes, his arresting good looks, or the subtle challenge that seemed just underneath the surface of his words. "I do, but I'm not…I mean I'm trained, but I don't do it for a living."

"Why not?" He stood and put on his white double breasted chef's jacket.

He seemed more intimidating at his full height, making her briefly wonder if she was crazy to try to help him. But he'd seemed so helpless only a few minutes ago. Now he looked as if he could lift three hundred pounds without breaking a sweat. "I already have a job and I'm a little out of practice."

"You can practice on me."

"What?"

"Or I'll pay you."

"What?"

"I like what you can do."

Clarice began to shake her head then stopped when he lowered his head looking both fierce and vulnerable at the same time. The way he did it reminded her of something. No…of *someone*. "Wait, why do you seem familiar?"

He shrugged. "I don't know."

"Have we met before?"

He shoved on his outer jacket. "I don't think so."

"But you may know our food." Theo held out a card. "Delites Bakery. We can make any occasion delicious."

She looked at the card then up at the man. And the image of a wedding feast flashed through her mind, pictures on her desk, an invoice and a young man who'd asked her out. Although she didn't think she'd get any offers from the man standing in front of her now. What was his name again? She may not remember that, but she did remember him. In eight years he had filled out and his appearance matched his voice. The fuzz of a mustache was gone replaced by broad shoulders and a chiseled jaw.

It wasn't just his cakes that looked delicious. He looked edible too, like a smooth chocolate ice cream bar. But perhaps he didn't remember her. Or felt embarrassed by his youthful ardor and he wanted to pretend that he didn't. She decided not to press the issue. "The cake looked amazing and tasted even better."

The young boy smiled wide, pumping out his chest in pride. "Thanks," he said.

The man didn't smile or show much emotion as if her compliment bored him. He'd likely grown used to them by now. "Well, I'd better go. Thanks again." He opened the door. "Come on, Theo."

"At least I accomplished one thing," Clarice said. "I'd always wanted to taste something you'd made and now I'm disappointed."

He spun around too fast and winced. "Disappointed?"

She reached for him then drew her hands back. "Be careful, you're still sore. Don't move so quickly."

He took a step towards her, trapping her in his gaze. "Disappointed?"

She tilted her head to the side and grinned; pleased she'd been able to provoke him as she had in the past. "So it is you?" she asked ready to hear him admit it.

He didn't take the bait. "What do you mean you were disappointed?"

She shoved her hands in the pockets of her skirt and nodded her head. "Yes. I'm disappointed that I had to wait so long to taste one of the best cakes I've ever had. You've got a gift."

"I know. I studied and everything."

"He means thanks," Theo said.

"No, it means 'I know' and I still don't know what you're talking about."

"I don't blame you," Clarice said with a dismissive wave of her hand. "You were young and it was a long time ago. I don't blame you for forgetting me."

He nodded and left.

Theo stayed behind. "He's not always like that. He can be nice too."

Clarice smiled at the boy not wanting him to be anxious. "I understand. He's still hurting and doesn't want to admit it."

Theo nodded. "Yea, that's it. Don't forget us. The bakery's address is on the card and you can see what we have online."

"I will and since you gave me your card, here's mine including my cell phone number. Call me any time."

He grinned, taking the card from her. "Thanks. We do cookies too and brownies that will—"

"Theo!" the man called from the hallway.

"I'd better go before I get into trouble."

"No, we wouldn't want that." She lightly cupped his cheek. "No matter what he says, you did the right thing by asking me to help you."

The anxiety that had hovered behind the little boy's eyes disappeared. He waved goodbye then dashed off. Clarice couldn't stop a smile. Just as she had felt all those years ago she was a little sad to see him go.

Chapter Five

Theo looked up at his uncle as they made their way towards the exit of the rental hall. "Are you still hurting really bad?"

"Why?"

"'Cause she was nice and you treated her like that."

"Like what?"

He motioned to the door of the utility closet. "Like that."

"You still have to be more specific."

"Like the others. Like the ones who like you. The ones who come by the shop and giggle and say 'Oh Drew'," he said, mimicking the ladies high tones.

He shrugged. "It wasn't intentional."

"I hope she'll remember the card."

"We don't need the business."

"Yes, we do. I overheard you talking that we couldn't turn anyone away because money's tight."

Drew pushed the front door open and squinted at the sunlight. His gaze swept the parking lot and noticed the Delites delivery van was missing then quickly remembered he'd sent the staff away after delivering the cake. He hadn't wanted them to worry about him.

"And I liked her," Theo continued as Drew used his cell phone to get a driver to pick them up. "I think she's buttercream."

"She's too old for you."

Theo rolled his eyes. "I know that, but she'd make a good client. She looks like she has money."

Drew agreed, but didn't want to say so. Why the hell did he have to see her again when he was at his most vulnerable? God how pathetic he must have looked writhing on the floor in pain, squeezing back tears of agony? Just as she had done years ago, she'd turned him into putty in her hands.

She looked even more refined and beautiful than she had eight years ago. More out of his league. Although he wasn't really sure what league he was in. He'd been with enough women to know he had varied taste. She had hands that worked magic. He wanted to see her again, feel her again, purely for professional reasons of course. She was good at what she did.

He didn't want to remember the amusement on her face when he'd asked her out all those years ago. He'd been bolder and more impulsive then. He was more cautious now. Plus, he rarely had to do the asking. Women came to him.

But she didn't look like someone who would come to him easily. Was she married now? He hadn't felt or noticed a ring. In truth he was in too much pain to notice much of anything at first. It was a slow dawning as her hands kneaded his muscles, as she spoke softly to him, as a familiar scent—a woodsy floral scent—that took him back to the young man he'd once been and how much he'd wanted to know her better.

Was she seeing someone? If so, why did he care? He was seeing someone too. Jennifer was the woman in his life now. The woman he saw in his future. Clarice Yates was an infatuation from his past.

But his pride still wanted to erase the day and change it. If he could have orchestrated another meeting, she would have been his client and he would have given her a cake she'd never forget. And he'd stay to watch her white teeth sink into the soft yellow layers of a lemon cake; he'd wait long enough to see her lick icing from her lips.

"Why did she think she knew you?"

Drew glanced back at the rental hall hoping that the party would last longer so that Clarice wouldn't come out and find them standing there. "I have that kind of face."

"You sure you don't remember her?"

I remember her. "I'm sure."

"It's just that…"

"What?"

"You looked at her funny."

"Funny?"

"Yes, when she talked about being disappointed with the cake you didn't look angry like you usually would, but you looked..." Theo scratched his head and shrugged his shoulders. "I don't know. Hurt."

Drew silently swore, heat burning his cheeks, embarrassed that his nephew had noticed and hoping she hadn't noticed too. Damn, all these years and her opinion still mattered? He didn't even know her really, why would it matter? But it did. He just wanted to be the only one who knew it. "I was hurt. I was in pain because I turned too fast. Nothing else."

Theo nodded. "Yea, that must be it. I told you I thought you looked funny." He shifted from one foot to the other then back again. "Do you think she—"

"Let's change the subject."

"But I just wanted to say one more thing."

"You can tell me tomorrow."

"But what if I forget?"

"Then it wasn't really important."

Theo sighed. "All right. Never mind."

Yes, that was the problem. He still did.

He couldn't sleep. Didn't want to sleep. Was afraid to sleep and dream of Clarice's hands sliding over his shoulders and back, taking him from hell into heaven. Drew lay in bed, surrounded by darkness, listening to the sound of someone dumping glass bottles into the recycling bin out back of his apartment complex.

"One of the best cakes I've ever had. You've got a gift." Yes, and her words stopped him from sleeping too. They kept repeating in his mind and he liked the way they made him feel, which didn't make sense. He should be used to compliments by now, but her words…

"Stuart, can you believe this?" Drew whispered into the dark, talking to a brother who could no longer answer back. "What is wrong with me? What is going on? I haven't felt this way since…I don't think I've ever felt this way."

He didn't know why he couldn't put a name to the feeling. Proud? No, he was always proud of what he created. Validated? No, his business had given him plenty of that, as well as the steady stream of referrals. Happy? Yes, that was it, but even that didn't make complete sense. He'd been complimented plenty of times, but somehow the tone of her words, the look in her eyes seemed to penetrate him, touch him to his core the way no one else could.

You've got a gift. He rubbed his chin thoughtful. Did she mean it or was she just teasing him again? He'd never forget how she'd tricked him by pretending she wouldn't pay the invoice then handed him the full amount. He remembered the sparkle of humor in her gaze. He'd noticed that sparkle now, but she also seemed genuine and he knew he was one of the best. *The* best, if he wanted to be honest. His business just wasn't at the financial level to prove it yet. He was still just breaking even every month no matter how hard he worked and he couldn't figure out why.

His good mood slowly slipped away as the realities of his life came into view. He had to provide for his nephew, the product of his brother's brief and sad marriage to a woman who didn't want to be a wife or mother and Theo had no contact with her side of the family. Drew had promised his brother that Theo would always be provided for no matter what and Stuart trusted him, which was why Drew had been made guardian over their parents.

But Drew didn't know how much longer he could hold up under the struggle of keeping the business afloat. The back spasm hadn't been the first time his body had failed him. But, except for Theo, he kept that to himself not wanting to worry anyone.

He wished Clarice would take him up on his offer to provide professional massages. His body had never felt so loose. But he knew that was wishful thinking.

But then again, meeting her had changed his life eight years ago when he was nineteen going on twenty. He'd seen his boss, Gerry Montrose, in the back office of the bakery looking grim. Although Drew preferred to be in the kitchen, he liked to also pay attention to the other aspect of running a bakery and asked questions about the business every chance he got. He'd started working there at fourteen in the summers, and almost six years later, he was still curious to know every aspect of the business and Gerry was always patient to oblige.

Gerry, a man with a push broom mustache and bald brown head, had bought the bakery after retiring from a corporate job. His wife did catering on the side and they blended their efforts, but more than once, Drew had overheard that the catering jobs were the only things keeping the bakery going, despite its prime location and good food. "What's wrong?" Drew asked, seeing Gerry wipe his forehead with a cloth.

Gerry sat back in his chair and sighed. "The Yates-Siggins affair still hasn't been paid. I'll have to swallow the costs. It's going to hurt."

Drew frowned. "Why would you do that? Just ask them to pay."

Gerry shook his head. "We're dealing with accountants. They're the worse. They'll nickel and dime you to death."

"But we fulfilled the contract," Drew said indignant. "We should get paid."

"Things are tight right now. We've already lost enough business because of the recession. It's not worth spending the effort."

"I'll do it."

"You'll do what?"

"I'll get them to pay."

Gerry couldn't help a grin. "I remember being as naïve as you once."

Drew stiffened. He didn't think he was naïve, he knew what was right. He knew people were hurting, but so were they. "I can do this. But what will I get in return?"

Gerry's brows shot up. "You want to make an agreement?"

He nodded.

Gerry thought for a moment, smoothing out his mustache. "If you get them to pay the full amount, that means no discounts, no payment plans, nothing but the full check." He paused for dramatic effect. "Then I'll give you the bakery."

Drew didn't move.

"Did you hear what I said?"

"I'm not sure I can believe it."

Gerry laughed. "Believe it. If you can make this happen this bakery is yours. You've worked here long enough, got the skills and you are at the legal age."

"Thank you."

"I haven't given it to you yet. Plus business isn't that great. You'd be staying on board a sinking ship."

"I don't care." He held out his hand.

Gerry shook it. "You will."

But he didn't. Clarice paid him the full amount and he was able to wave a check in front of Gerry's stunned face. "I don't believe this," Gerry said in wonder. "What the hell did you do?"

"Just worked my charm."

"I guess if I were as young and as good looking as you, I'd get lucky too. I should have thought of sending you out before."

"Are you going to keep your word?"

Gerry ran a hand down his face. "My wife's going to kill me, but I gave you my word."

"We can be co-owners."

"With you having the bigger percentage?"

"Of course."

"Okay," Gerry said looking relieved as he shook Drew's hand.

"Now that we're partners, I'll make sure that we always get paid."

In the intervening years, Drew did more than that. He helped to turn things around. Even though business continued to squeak by into the black, it didn't stay in the red as it had before. He'd helped Delites pay off its loans, gave Gerry time to spend with his family and slowly helped the name grow, giving it a stellar online presence and contemporary vibe.

But over the past two years things had stagnated and he couldn't figure out why. At times he wondered if it was because he now owned the business completely, after Gerry decided to semi-retire and give him full ownership. He still helped Drew with the bookkeeping and gave him ideas, but spent more time away. Although, unlike many other bakeries that had come and gone, Delites was still around, it hovered just above the survival stage.

At times Drew wondered if his luck had run out.

You've got a gift.

Clarice's words put a reluctant smile on his face. They weren't special words, but just what he needed to hear today. For some strange reason he felt that meeting Clarice again meant his luck was about to change.

Chapter Six

Drew woke to the sound of scratching against his door and a soft cry. He went to the back door of his ground level apartment, which led out to the back part of the property. He opened the door and saw a dog. A little Bichon Frise named Lady to be exact. The sight of her didn't surprise him. Lady came to his apartment to escape, since presently she lived in the middle of a war. She hadn't started it, but bore the brunt of the animosity of the two sides. Drew felt in the middle too.

In the middle of two neighbors who'd been living together when he'd first moved in three years ago, but had recently broken up. He thought of them as Bran Muffin (the man) and Lemon Ripple Cheesecake (the woman). They'd both frequented his bakery in the early days and had seemed an odd pair, but pleasant. Drew didn't know the real reason for their separation although he'd been given two different versions. She said Bran Muffin was a cheating, tightwad; he called Lemon Ripple a money-spending, paranoid. Whatever the reason, she moved out of the apartment. But not to another building, that would have been too easy, instead she moved to an apartment right above Drew's.

At one of the community parties the complex held, when they were still living together, Drew had warned them about getting a dog together, sharing some horror stories he'd heard from a friend. But they'd been so in love two years ago that nothing could talk them out of it.

Six months ago everything had gone to rot. Drew had heard the shouting in the hallway, the slamming front door, the breaking glass when a vase flew out the window (Bran Muffin said it was an accident because it was sitting on the ledge and he knocked it over; Lemon Ripple was convinced he'd done it on purpose).

And then it was over. Silence returned. They agreed he got to stay in the apartment; she got to keep the TV.

But the dog.

The dog started a new battle.

They both loved her for different reasons and neither wanted to give up custody. So they shuttled the dog between residences.

And it had worked fine for a couple of months until that all changed when Lemon Ripple asked Drew to look after Lady for several days. She didn't want to put her in a pet hotel or leave her with her ex. "He'd use it as a reason he should keep her more often. Please. I don't want to give him an excuse that I'm a bad parent."

"You realize Lady isn't a child, right?" Drew said.

She ignored him. "Please, just this once."

To his regret, Drew had agreed. He liked Lady and so did Theo. Gladys, an older woman Drew had hired to look after his nephew and keep the apartment clean, didn't at first. She was related to some second cousin on his father's side from Antigua and didn't like animals, 'All they do is create mess' she liked to say. But soon Lady won her over as well.

But within a few days Lady wasn't acting the same. She didn't want to be touched and winced if she was. She didn't want to go out for walks and seemed listless, but when Theo noticed blood coming from her mouth, Drew called Bran Muffin, but only got voice mail so he took her to see a vet. After visits to two vets—one who suggested Drew put Lady down—Drew discovered that Lady's skin was filled with sores and that she'd had an allergic reaction to something.

So Drew, still unable to contact Bran Muffin and not wanting to scare Lemon Ripple, had to put the little dog on an elimination diet and learned that she'd been allergic to the high quality gourmet dog food his neighbor had been giving her.

Drew had felt pleased, and relieved when Lemon Ripple returned and he told her the outcome.

"I'm not paying for this vet bill," she said, looking at the bill Drew handed her, when she came to pick up Lady. "Tell him to cover it."

"Come on," Drew said in disbelief.

"He's the one who told me that we should give her the same food so that she could have a regular diet. I wasn't the one who initially poisoned her. He chose the brand. Did you know that he's dating some girl at the pet store? I'm sure he only bought this expensive brand to impress her. He never buys expensive things."

"I'm sure it was an honest mistake."

"That *I* didn't make."

When Drew gave the bill to Bran Muffin, he also shook his head. "No way is she putting this on me. She's the one who didn't like the initial no name brand. Ask her. Ask her how many different brands we've gone through already."

Drew didn't ask, but after that incident the war was on. For the past few weeks there had been the return of slamming doors and "I'll see you in court" and the little dog made her way to Drew's door without anyone noticing until days passed and either Bran Muffin or Lemon Ripple arrived on Drew's doorstep to collect her.

Drew looked down at the dog, a cute cloud of curly white hair, wondering how long it would take them this time. He let the dog in and stroked her. "Poor girl. Think Lemon Ripple will notice you're gone?" Lady looked up at him with sad brown eyes. He sighed. "Me neither." Drew straightened and the dog walked over to the water bowl and food Drew left out for her in the kitchen.

Theo came out of his bedroom and smiled when he saw the dog. "I didn't know Lady was here." He knelt by the dog and stroked her. "Can't we keep her?"

"I told you she's not ours."

"But they're so mean to her."

"You can ask."

Theo looked suddenly shy. "She scares me."

"You can ask him."

Theo stood and wrung his hands. "I think he's scared of her too."

"Then when they come to get her, you have to let her go."

"But you could ask her. Women like you."

Drew shook his head. "No, if you want Lady, you do something about it. Have you eaten?"

He nodded. "Ms. Gladys left you some banana porridge."

Drew inwardly shivered. Gladys could clean, but cooking wasn't her strong point. Fortunately, Theo didn't notice. If someone added enough sugar or salt he'd eat it.

"Maybe if I offer to buy him."

Drew opened the fridge. "Maybe."

"How much do you think she'll cost?"

He grabbed an egg. "I don't know."

Theo looked thoughtful for a moment then raced out of the room and returned with a card. He took Drew's cell phone from the table and began to dial.

Drew grabbed a bowl. "You're calling her now?"

"No, I'm calling Ms. Yates."

"What?" Drew said, dropping the egg he'd meant to crack over the bowl.

Theo turned away from him and began to speak, "Hello? Is this Ms.—hey!" he cried when Drew snatched the phone from him.

"You can't call her."

"Why not?"

"B-because you don't ask strangers to solve your problems." Drew set the cell phone back on the table, grabbed several paper towels and cleaned up the ruined egg.

"Yes, you do. If your house is on fire you call a firefighter. If you get robbed you call the police. If your house is dirty you get a housecleaner. If your—"

Drew threw the mess away and washed his hands. "All right. All right you have a point, but do you have the money to pay her for her advice?"

Theo sat at the kitchen table and reached for the cell phone. "I just wanted to ask a question."

Drew moved it out of reach. "People like her charge by the minute."

He sank into his seat. "Really?"

Drew nodded.

The phone rang.

Theo straightened and pointed. "That's probably her. You have to answer."

"She can leave a message."

He jumped to his feet. "Can't I just talk to her?"

"No."

The phone stopped ringing.

Theo's shoulders sagged. "Why won't you let me get my own phone?"

"Because you don't need one yet. You'll get your own in two years."

He dropped into his chair and made a face. "Two more years is forever."

"It will go by in a flash."

"All my friends—"

"I don't care."

"I wouldn't talk long. She said I could call and ask her anything."

Drew's tone sharpened. "When did she say that?"

"Before we left."

"She was just being polite." Drew opened the fridge again and reached for another egg then thought better of it and closed the door. He looked at his nephew. "Don't bother her. Okay?"

Theo sent a longing look at Lady who was now tugging on one of her favorite toys—a rag doll.

Drew glanced at the cell phone, feeling a twinge of guilt. Why had he felt such a moment of panic? What was the harm in Theo asking her a simple question?

Drew started to say, I'll see what I can do about Lady, but stopped when the doorbell rang.

"Who is it?" he called out.

"It's me," a soft feminine voice replied.

Theo's eyes widened. "Oh no, it's Jennifer." He jumped up and turned.

Drew grabbed him by the collar before he could run away. "Where do you think you're going?"

"I've…I've got some homework to do."

"It can wait." He walked to the door with Theo in tow.

Theo struggled against him. "Please Uncle Drew don't make me say hi. She keeps calling me Teddy."

"Maybe she won't this time." He opened the door and smiled. "Hey baby."

Jennifer kissed him lightly on the lips. "Hey back at ya." She held up a brown bag. "I bought some breakfast."

"Thanks."

She rubbed Theo's head. "Hey there, Teddy."

He shot his uncle an 'I-told-you-so' glance.

"His name is Theo," Drew said.

"I know, but he reminds me of a cute teddy."

Theo curled his lip. "Can I go to my room now?"

"Yes."

He stomped away.

"You shouldn't do that," Drew said letting her in.

"Do what?"

He hung up her orange jacket in the hall closet. It matched the headband in her brown shoulder length hair. "He doesn't like being treated like a kid."

"But he is a kid."

"Okay, then let me rephrase that. He doesn't like being treated like a five-year-old." He walked to the kitchen.

"But he is *soooo* cute," Jennifer said, setting the brown bag on the table.

"Honey, I warned you about that," Drew said, struggling to keep his voice tender, although he was beginning to get as irritated as his nephew. "If you want this relationship to work, Theo is part of it and there are certain boundaries. You respect that he wants to be called Theo."

"All right." She pulled out two circular shaped aluminum wrapped items. "You look a little tired. Have you been working all night again?"

Drew sat across the table from her. "No."

"Don't forget your promise."

He slowly unwrapped the item she'd pushed towards him. It smelled like an egg and cheese melt. "Promise?"

"Another six months and then you sell the bakery."

"Yes, I wanted to talk to you about that."

"What's there to talk about?"

He stared down at his breakfast. "I want another two years." He met her gaze, hoping she'd understand. "If I can get a loan—"

Jennifer shook her head. "You said—"

"I know what I said but I felt pressured at the time. I didn't think I would be able to keep the bakery going as well as looking after Theo." He'd made the rash promise nearly a year ago when his world felt like it was going to fall apart. She'd been there for him and he didn't want to lose her too, so he'd told her what he knew she'd wanted to hear. But now that his life was getting a little more settled, he'd had second thoughts.

She stood and grabbed a glass from the cupboard. "Has something changed?" She poured herself some orange juice. "Are you suddenly making more money or something?"

"Not yet, but—"

She returned to the table. "For the past eighteen months I've watched you work your behind off, but you're still not creating the kind of traction you need to have a successful business. You told me you've been working at this for eight years. Isn't that long enough?"

"No. I'm not ready to quit yet. I'm too close."

She took a sip of her juice then slowly set it down. "Too close to what?"

I don't know. Something. "I need two more years."

"I've been patient and understanding, haven't I? The early mornings, the late nights. The big events and small ones. I've stood by your side, especially after..." She let her words fade away. "But if we want a future together we have to be realistic. You're still young enough to do whatever you want."

"I want to bake cakes."

"Be serious."

"You know I am. You knew this is what I did when you met me."

She sighed. "I know and I love you. I just…I don't want to see you get hurt in case it doesn't work out."

"I don't mind failing. But I don't want to quit too soon." He reached across the table and covered her hand. "Just give me a little more time," he said in a soft voice, Clarice's face and encouraging words drifted through his mind. "I think this is going to be my best year yet."

Chapter Seven

That was strange, Clarice thought as she stood in her dining room and stared down at her cell phone. She'd returned from visiting her sister, buying groceries and had just replied to some funny texts from her father who always made her smile, when her phone rang and a child's voice began to speak then cut off. When she'd called the number she'd seen displayed, she'd been surprised and a little thrilled to hear Drew's recorded voice message come on the line. "Yes, this is Drew. You know what to do."

For a moment she didn't, and ended up leaving a rather awkward message. "Hi, Drew…I mean Theo. I don't know if we got disconnected, but I believe you called me. Again my number is…." She hung up wondering if he would. A part of her hoping he would and another part fearing it.

You can practice on me. That was an offer she couldn't get out of her head. She really loved giving massage. She hadn't realized how much she'd missed it until she'd helped him. It was her true passion. She'd dreamed of owning a spa, or even doing freelance. The day of her mother's wedding, she'd planned to tell her mother that her teacher had offered her a position. That Luisa had been so impressed with her that she thought Clarice could become one of the tops in the field.

But then her mother's heart had been broken and Clarice had also buried her dreams with it. But now she had been given two chances within a week. First, meeting Luisa again and the possibility of having to take a skills test to get a possible job and now a chance to practice on someone.

She hadn't practiced in a while and if she wanted to impress her former teacher this was her chance. Plus, although she continued taking courses online to keep current, there were so many hands-on aspects she wanted to try. And Drew had the perfect build for it. Not too fat, not too thin but just right. *Mr. Right*, her naughty mind whispered before she pushed the thought away.

No, she wasn't interested in him as a man, but as a teaching tool, a learning opportunity. Maybe if she just did a massage session two more times, just to make sure she still had the knack, she'd get the desire out of her system and then remember that she was fine where she was.

But you know you want this, her traitorous mind whispered again. *It was fun, invigorating. Touching him made you feel alive.*

Clarice shook her head, pushing the thought aside. *Stop it.* She wasn't going to go on the interview and she wasn't going to do massage. Her life didn't need any more drama.

By the middle of the following week, she'd forgotten about the strange phone call, until she received another call from the same number as she'd started closing down the office.

She answered and again heard a child's voice then the phone disconnected. Was Theo playing some weird game?

When it happened a third time, she decided to call back right away.

"Hello?" Drew said.

"What is wrong with him?" Clarice asked.

"With who?"

"Theo. Why does he keep calling and hanging up? Couldn't he just leave a message? Send a text?"

"I don't know what you mean. The first time my nephew called you was by mistake. I apologize."

"What about the other two times?"

He paused. "What other times?"

Clarice immediately felt guilty. Clearly Theo had been trying to reach her without his uncle knowing. She'd remembered how nervous he'd been when she'd first met him. Maybe he was concerned about his uncle's health and wanted to talk to her privately. Whatever the reason she didn't want him to get into trouble. "Never mind. It's nothing."

Drew's voice hardened. "I told him not to bother you."

"He didn't. I—"

But she stopped when she heard him call Theo's name. She didn't want him to get into trouble so she quickly said, "Drew, wait!"

"What?"

"I must have gotten confused. I'm sure it was just the one missed call. Actually, I'd wanted to talk to you."

"Really? Why?"

Clarice swallowed scrambling her mind for a good reason. Why would she call him? "I'm just calling to see how you're doing."

"I'm fine."

She hesitated. He sounded a lot more distant on the phone and about as cuddly as a steel covered porcupine. Maybe this wasn't a good idea. "Well, that's good to know. Have you seen a doctor?"

He didn't reply.

A steel covered porcupine with lethal claws. It wouldn't be easy to manipulate him now. She needed to end the call. "Well, I guess—"

"What do you want?"

"What?"

"You didn't just call me to find out how I'm doing. You were angry."

"No, not angry confused. I don't get angry really easy, actually. My family thinks I'm really mellow." *Dear God she was babbling. Get yourself together Clarice. You've dealt with your mother. You can deal with a surly man.* "Actually, the truth is I had to gather my courage to take you up on your offer." She squeezed her eyes closed. *What was she saying?* She usually wasn't so impulsive. That was her sister's territory.

She would have said yes the first moment he'd asked and given him a fee and time. She'd learned early to be cautious.

"My offer?"

Oh no did he forget? Was that just a joke? "Yes." She cleared her throat. If she was going to be nuts she might as well go all the way. "To let you practice on me?" She shook her head. "I mean to let *me* practice on *you*. Massage," she clarified. "Remember?" She waited. Maybe he'd pretend to forget, just as he'd pretended not to remember her from all those years ago. That would probably be for the best. *Just forget about me so that I can hang up and pretend this conversation never happened.*

"Yes," he said in a low voice.

"But clearly you're busy and…I'm sorry," she said when she heard him mumble something. "What did you say?"

"When can you start?"

She paused, her heart starting to race. Was he serious? He really wanted to do this? She closed her eyes again. *Clarice this isn't good. You'd lied to him about the reason you'd called to get the kid out of trouble. Now you're getting into it instead. Just give him a date and an amount he'd have to refuse.*

"Is your schedule that busy?" he said, a little impatient.

"Yes," she lied. "How about next Wednesday at seven?"

"Can you make it eight-thirty?"

Say no and then you can get out of this. "Sure," she said instead.

"Good. You can come to my place." He rattled off an address then hung up.

Clarice stared at the phone. *You idiot!* What have you done? You can't do this. You can't use him as practice. He was taciturn and brusque. But then on the other hand she didn't need him to be friendly. He would just be an instrument. No, that wasn't the right term. A mannequin.

He could be the key to another life at last. What if she did pass the skills test and got to work with Luisa? What if she did and it slowly expanded into other jobs? Maybe this was her chance and it was time to stop being afraid.

Clarice looked around the light tan walls in her office. It was an even toned hue that mirrored her even toned life. Drew could be her chance to escape this. To be the person she'd once dreamed she could be. She clasped her hands together. For the first time in years she didn't feel as if she were dying inside. Helping Drew and practicing for the skills test would be just a small taste of freedom.

Chapter Eight

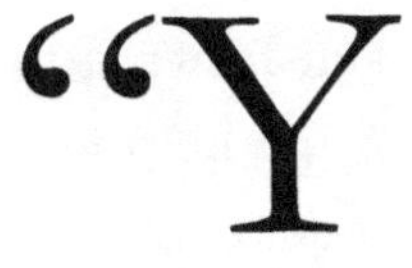

"You're a very lucky kid," Drew said as he faced Theo in the living room that evening after dinner.

"I am?"

"Yes, because today I'm not going to get angry at you for calling Ms. Yates when I told you not to."

"You're not?"

"No."

"And do you want to know why?"

He nodded.

Drew turned on the TV. "Too bad because I'm not going to tell you."

"But—"

Drew shot him a glance. "Do you want me to be angry?"

Theo quickly shook his head.

"Then let's forget this happened."

"Okay." Theo rubbed his hands on his jeans. Lady lay at his feet. Her owners still hadn't noticed her absence. "Was she angry?"

"About what? About you calling her and hanging up?"

He nodded.

"I'm not going to tell you that either." He pointed. "I'm letting you off easy, but let this be a lesson to you."

Theo nodded again before he shuffled away.

Drew sat back and sighed amazed at himself. Amazed that he wasn't angry. Amazed that he looked forward to Clarice's visit. She could help him. If she could help him stay limber without anyone knowing, he could make it through the busy spring and summer season.

Two days later a package arrived at his door.

"What is it?" Theo asked as they stared at the package Gladys had left on the kitchen counter.

"I don't know."

"You didn't order it?"

"No."

"I wonder who it's from." Theo made a face. "Think it's from Jennifer?"

Drew playfully tweaked his nephew's nose. "If it is, I'm sure it's nice."

Drew looked at the return address surprised. "Ms. Yates," he said then opened the box and laughed as he pulled out a gift box of herbal teas—mango passion fruit, peppermint, chamomile and wild raspberry hibiscus. He read the note: *Bet you don't remember this either.* "Oh, you cruel woman," he said, remembering how adamantly he'd told her his tea preference years ago.

Theo looked at the colorful boxes and sighed. "Oh no. She doesn't know how much you hate them."

"Yes, she does."

"Then why did she send them?"

"Just because," he said, not in the mood to explain something that suddenly seemed special.

Theo stroked Lady as she snuggled beside him on the bed. He couldn't remember the last time he'd seen his uncle laugh out loud like that. Those teas had made him happy even though he knew his uncle hated herbal teas. Maybe it wasn't the tea. Maybe it was Ms. Yates. Yeah, that was it. Ms. Yates had made his uncle happy just like she'd helped him when he got hurt.

Theo wished he'd gotten a chance to talk to her. He was sure she could help him with Lady. Ms. Yates was so much better than Jennifer. He bet she'd never call him Teddy. Or ask his uncle to close the bakery.

Gladys liked her and so did his grandparents and she could be nice…but…Ms. Yates just seemed nicer. He closed his eyes hoping she'd visit the bakery. Maybe she'd like the food so much she'd stop by lots of times and maybe one time he'd get a chance to see her again.

Clarice was finishing up with work and thinking of the TV dinner she'd pop in the oven (she could microwave it but using the oven made her feel she was at least making an effort) when her phone rang. The number surprised her.

"Hello, Drew. How can I—"

"I need to reschedule," he said in a tight voice.

She furrowed her brows, worried by his tone. "Reschedule?"

"Yeah, my appointment."

"Is something wrong?"

"Yes," he said through ground teeth. "I really need you tonight."

Chapter Nine

He needed her *tonight?* But she wasn't ready. Clarice shook her head, brushing her worries aside. It didn't matter if he was in pain. She knew he wasn't the kind of man to reach out for help unless he really needed it. "Another back spasm?"

"Hmm."

"How bad is it?"

"Bad enough."

"Did you fall again?"

"No…these things happen. Can you come or not?"

She checked the time then searched for his address. "Yes, but—"

"I'm not too far from your office."

"But your apartment is—"

"I'm not there. I'm at the bakery. I'll be waiting in the back." He hung up.

First a utility closet and now the back of a bakery? What was wrong with this man? Clarice quickly gathered her things and sighed. She wanted to help him. She'd even gotten a portable massage bed which she'd left in her car never expecting she'd need it in an emergency.

When she arrived at the bakery it was dim and quiet. "Hello?" she called, but no one answered. She made her way to the back. To her relief instead of finding him on the floor, he lay on a cot. Unfortunately, everything else was the same—the tense jaw, the sheen of sweat, the body twisted in pain. He rolled his eyes towards her then looked away again.

She'd brought her massage bed, but didn't think she'd be able to get him to move.

"I brought oil this time so it may get a little messy and the sheets—"

He stared at the ceiling. "I don't care. Do what you need to."

She plugged in a heating pad. He winced and swore when he was forced to move so that she could place it underneath him.

"What's that for?" he growled.

"To help with the inflammation. You'll thank me in a minute," she said then started to knead his thigh, working her way up to his hips.

He moaned.

She paused. "Am I hurting you anywhere? Anywhere especially tender?"

"No."

She started again and he moaned once more, but he made a quick, short motion with his head. "No, don't stop. That's it. You hit the spot. God, I need that."

Clarice sighed; glad to give him some relief, but she knew it wasn't enough. "I'm going to need you to turn over and lie face down."

He briefly closed his eyes. "Can't you just kill me first?"

"Take a deep breath and then it will be over."

It took more than one deep breath. Moving him lasted much longer than both of them would have wished, but finally he was positioned so that she could massage the places that caused him the most pain. She'd sensed the flare up would occur in the same location as last time and found it again.

"God," he said in a deep shuddering breath. "I just need it to stop."

Clarice focused on his tender spot. "I'm not going to let you win tonight," she said, talking to the tense muscle. "You're going to surrender. Do you hear me?"

She selected some oil then slowly slid her hands along the length of his back, training and intuition guiding her to know where to place pressure and where to go gently.

She kneaded his muscles and as they had before, they surrendered to her touch and slowly tension melted away.

He groaned. "Yes, that's right. That's what I need."

"Drew—"

"Shh…don't speak. Let your hands do the talking. And right now they're saying all that I want to hear."

Clarice worked until his breathing became more even. Soon she felt him drift off to sleep. She hated to wake him, but didn't want to leave him sleeping alone in the back of an open shop. She nudged him awake. "Drew?"

"Hmm?"

"I'm done."

"Okay, thanks."

She stood. "Will you be all right here?"

"Hmm."

That means yes, she could imagine Theo telling her.

She covered him with a sheet and then turned off the lights. "Sweet dreams," she whispered before she left.

Drew woke up from a dream into a nightmare.

He'd emerged from thoughts of soft hands and whipped cream to the sound of steel pots clattering together and shouting.

He followed the sounds into the kitchen then halted dumbfounded at the sight before him—his staff trying to restrain an enraged Jennifer.

Before he could speak, one of his staffers shouted, "No! Not the cake!" but his plea came too late as she toppled the four tiered pink champagne cake to the ground.

Chapter Ten

His girlfriend had clearly gone insane.

But he'd deal with her temporary madness later. Right now he had to fix a disaster. He pointed to his stunned staff and gave directions. It was early enough to keep things running, there were enough baked items for the morning crowd and the cake wasn't due to be delivered to a client for another several hours. "Clear this up. Use what we'd started for our evening affair for this one. Move!" They jumped into action trying to create what had taken five hours in three.

Drew dragged Jennifer, who had been staring at the ruined cake in triumph, out of the kitchen and into the hall that separated it from his back office. "Is this psychotic episode a fluke or something I should get used to?" he said in a low voice.

She yanked herself free from him. "Don't you dare make fun of me."

"I'm not in the mood to make fun. I want to know what the hell is going on."

"You tell me."

"If you have a problem with me, you know where I live. You deal with me." He tapped his chest. "But you never take out your anger on my food. Ever. This is my business. I have a reputation to maintain."

She rolled her eyes and sniffed. "You didn't care about your reputation last night."

He frowned. "What?"

"I heard you last night. I knew you were working late because I spoke to Gladys, so I came here to surprise you and I heard you in the back."

"So what? You know I sometimes work late. I like the evening when it's quiet."

"You weren't working this time. I heard you! I heard all of it."

"Heard what?"

She folded her arms and glared at him. "You're really going to stare at me like you're innocent?"

"Because I am innocent. I don't know what you're talking about."

"You weren't alone."

Drew blinked then swore as he remembered his session with Clarice. "No. Wait. That's not—"

Penny, his head baker, came out holding a tiny gold hoop earring. "I was sweeping the office and found this under your cot."

Jennifer glared at him. "Your cot? Is that where you work late now?"

Drew shook his head. "No, it's not what you think." He knew it was a lame line, but didn't know what else to say. "Really, I—"

His words froze on his lips when he saw Clarice coming towards them.

"Your clerk at the front was kind enough to let me back here when I told her I'd left…" She noticed the earring in Penny's hand. "That's it! I knew I'd left it here. I've been looking all over for it. My sister would kill me if I lost it."

Drew swore.

Jennifer screamed. "I knew it!" She stared at him as she pointed to Clarice. "Are you going to deny it now?"

"Keep your voice down," Drew demanded. "And let me explain."

"No," she said, her voice cracking in anguish. "You want me to pretend you didn't break my heart?"

Drew held up his hands. "Jennifer, I know how it looks, but it's *really* not what you think."

"You weren't with that woman last night?"

"I was. She was giving me a massage."

Jennifer curled her lip, giving Clarice a once over. "Funny, she doesn't look like one of those. How much does she charge for office visits? Or do you pay her in cupcakes?"

"You're being ridiculous."

"I know what I heard."

"But did you see anything?"

"Of course not! Do you think I'd want to see you with another woman?"

"I wasn't with another woman and if you'd come in you would have seen that."

"But—"

"Jennifer," he said with thinning patience. "When have I ever lied to you?"

"Oh, so you're Jennifer," Clarice cut in before Jennifer could speak. "Drew has told me so much about you and he talked about you so much last night that I felt as if I knew you. I'm sorry for this silly misunderstanding, but he is telling the truth. Nothing happened. I'm a massage therapist. Board certified and licensed. He's a man to be trusted. You're very lucky."

She looked chagrined and touched her forehead in dismay. "Oh my God what have I done?"

Drew's temper snapped. "You—"

"It could have happened to anyone," Clarice interrupted, sending Drew a look to be quiet.

Jennifer let her hand fall. "You don't know what it's like," she said in a sad little voice. "There are so many women surrounding him. Always wanting a taste of him. Always teasing me about enjoying his samples. Telling me how they just can't get enough."

"The food is good."

"How much they want to lick his icing," she continued. Clarice cleared her throat. "Yes, well—"

Jennifer stared at something in the distance and gripped her hand into a fist. "I see the hunger in their eyes. And—"

Clarice snapped her fingers in front of Jennifer's face, jolting the younger woman out of her thoughts. "I only came last night because he hurt his—" She abruptly stopped when Drew nudged her in the side with his elbow. "Shoulder," she finished. "And he needed to be in top shape today. That's why he called me. Nothing more."

Jennifer turned to Drew and reached for his cheek with trembling fingers. "Oh, baby. I'm sorry."

He stepped away from her. "I'll talk to you later."

"I mean, what else was I supposed to think with all that moaning and groaning and 'yes that's what I need.' You don't even talk to me that way."

He took her by the shoulders and turned her to the front of the bakery. "I said we'll talk later. I've got to rescue this mess." He walked her to the entrance. She spun around and kissed him on the mouth before he could stop her. "I'll make it up to you," she said before she left.

"Somehow I knew coming here would be a bad idea," Clarice said as Drew walked past her.

"Not now," he said in a low voice.

"How can I help?"

"You can't."

She followed him to the kitchen and saw the staff cleaning up. She took off her coat. "Yes, I can. I'll clean while you start whipping up a new batter or do whatever you do."

She took the broom from a burly looking man with a hair net.

Drew hesitated. "You sure?"

"Trust me," Clarice said with a smug grin. "Cleaning up messes is what I do best."

Chapter Eleven

His body was as tense as a pulled guitar string.

"You overdid it this week, didn't you?" Clarice said. This time she had Drew on her massage table and was using lemon oil on his back. After she'd helped him clean the kitchen, she'd told him she'd see him at their original scheduled date and time half expecting him to tell her that he was fine and didn't need it. Instead, he'd grunted consent, told her to make it nine o'clock, before he focused his attention back on a mixer.

Now he lay half naked on her massage bed in the quiet of his apartment living room. Theo was already in bed and when Clarice worried they might wake him, Drew assured her that his nephew could sleep through anything, plus the design of the apartment had Theo's bedroom far enough down the hall that he could run both a mixer and a garbage disposal in the kitchen and not wake him.

"I didn't have a choice."

She knew that was true. He couldn't tell a client that their order hadn't been ready because a mad girlfriend had ruined it. "Is everything okay between you two now?"

"I haven't talked to her yet. Been too busy trying to save my business."

"I'll talk to her again if—"

"It's fine."

"But—"

"Why are you doing this?"

"What?"

"Why are you practicing on me?"

She sighed, sweeping her hands across the breadth of his back. "Because I have a skills test next month. A former teacher of mine may hire me for a position working with seniors and I wanted to make sure I'm still good."

"Does that mean you'll quit your current job?"

"No. The hours aren't enough. Besides, I can't make a living at this."

"Of course you can. Isn't that why you got your license?"

Clarice blinked, amazed by how quickly he could make her feel vulnerable. She cleared her throat, gathering her composure. "What's made you so chatty this evening?"

"Last time you told me to focus on something beside the pain. I focused on you then and I'm focusing on you now."

"Are you in pain?"

"Not right now and don't change the subject."

"Any pain since the spasm?" she said, ignoring his request.

He sighed resigned. "No."

"But you still have some tender spots and tight muscles. I don't know if I'm doing you any good. A doctor could—"

"I've already seen a doctor. I know what I have."

She waited. When he didn't tell her she said, "What?"

"Axial Spondyloarthritis."

Clarice gave a low whistle instead of swearing, which she wanted to do. Axial spondyloarthritis or AS was a term used to describe the possible early stage of ankylosing spondylitis, a progressive, chronic and painful form of inflammatory arthritis that resulted in some of the joints and bones of the spine becoming fused together. "Why didn't you say anything before?" she asked, searching her mind for the damage she could have caused. "You should have told me."

"Don't sound so worried," Drew said with a note of cynical amusement. "I'm not so fragile that I can break."

"Do you have a relative with it?" she asked since a majority of sufferers did.

"No. I'm just one of the weird ones I guess."

That made her wonder about the diagnosis. Although ten percent of people with AS didn't have the gene it was also rare in blacks. But at least he'd gone to a doctor. "I'm sorry."

"So you see why I don't want anyone knowing. I have a very physical job. A job I love. I want to keep doing it as long as I can."

"Maybe if—"

"I didn't ask you here to fix my life or tell me how to live it."

"True."

He fell silent then said, "But thanks for caring and your help at the bakery the other day."

"It's partially my fault. Although she is a little over imaginative."

"Why?"

"The moment she saw me she should have known nothing was going on."

"Why? Because you wouldn't be seen with a baker?"

"No, because we don't exactly look like a pair. After meeting Jennifer…I knew."

"You knew what?"

She rubbed one shoulder. "I knew your tastes had changed," she said with a laugh, hoping to sound more nonchalant than she felt. She felt a little embarrassed she'd even mentioned the past.

"My tastes haven't changed," he said in a low voice. "I just like different flavors."

A knot rose in her throat. She swallowed, feeling suddenly warm. *Cut it out Clarice. He's just teasing you now. Remember to be a professional. You just want his body.* She looked down feeling her hands tremble against his skin. *No, you just need his body. His beautiful, strong body.* Her hands trembled some more. She clasped them together then flexed her fingers. She had to stop thinking about his body as anything but a teaching tool.

"What about you? Are you seeing anyone?"

"No."

"Any particular flavor you like?" he asked with a smile in his voice.

Right now lemon and chocolate were all she could think about. "Uh…no."

"Really? Tell me your type of man and I'll give you a flavor."

"Never really thought of it."

"Think about it now."

"Why?"

"Because I'm curious."

"Thoughtful. Funny."

He waited then said, "That's it?"

"I told you I haven't thought about it. I'll know him when I taste him." She shook her head and quickly corrected herself, stumbling over the words, "I mean see him. When I see him I'll know. He'll be someone I can trust."

Drew tensed.

"Did I hurt you?"

"No." He slowly relaxed. "I'm not a player."

"I didn't say you were."

"The way Jennifer talked you'd think I had women falling all over me."

"I don't blame them. I've licked the icing off your cake."

He chuckled. "Somehow you made that sound dirty."

Clarice giggled. "I know. If Jennifer heard me now, she'd really think we were having an affair. Just for fun I should start talking about the moist center of your vanilla cake, the soft rise of your—"

He cleared his throat. "Actually I think you'd better not."

"Oh sorry. Got a little carried away there." *Keep it together Clarice.*

"What's your favorite cake?"

"I don't have one."

"Probably red velvet."

"Don't know. I've never had it."

He sat up and looked at her. "What?"

"Don't jump up like that. You scared me."

He gaped at her. "You've never had red velvet cake?"

"No."

"Angel food?"

She shook her head.

"Lemon?"

"Nope."

"What did you have for your birthday as a kid?"

"Cookies and ice cream."

He blinked. "Every birthday?"

Clarice nodded. "Yes, Mom said cakes were messy. I think I once made a cake with my Dad using a cake mix. It was good."

"Then how would you know?"

"Know what?"

"You said my castle cake was the best cake you've ever tasted but if you've only eaten cake mix out of a box how would you know the difference?"

"Give me some credit. If a person lived on frozen strawberries, they should be able to tell the difference from ones fresh off the vine. I wasn't trying to flatter you. Now lie back down."

"No, I have to test something." He wrapped the sheet around his waist and stood. "Follow me."

"I don't have time for this," she said following him to the kitchen.

"It won't take long. Sit down and close your eyes."

"You want me to do a taste test? You want me to prove that my compliment was real?"

"Close your eyes, please."

She folded her arms. "Fine, your cake wasn't the best. Happy now?"

"Close. Your. Eyes."

She looked at the counter and saw her gift box of teas near his electric tea kettle. "You haven't even opened it yet."

"Nope."

The corner of her mouth kicked up in a grin. "You won't try just one?"

"I'd rather break out in hives. Now close your eyes."

She made a face then did as instructed. "I'll never forget you telling me how you're a black tea man," she said with a laugh.

"I still am."

"Black?"

"Shut up."

She smiled. "Do you only drink loose tea too?"

"No, I'm not a total purist."

"Surprising. What part of England are your parents from?" she asked. She had a great-aunt and cousin who lived there.

"The wet part."

"You're a lovely conversationalist," she said, her voice heavy with sarcasm.

"Yes, I like nature."

"I didn't say conservationist."

"I know and keep your eyes closed," he warned when she started to open them.

She shifted in her seat. "What are you doing?"

"You'll find out in a minute." A few moments later he said, "Open your eyes."

In front of her were four small plates with thin slices of cake. "These are all simple yellow cakes. Tell me which one you like best."

Clarice pointed to the one on the far left. "This one." She looked up at him bored. "Can I go now?"

Drew held out the fork.

"You're as ridiculous as your girlfriend."

He waved the fork at her.

She snatched it from him. "This is the last time I compliment a man on his food," she mumbled. She took a bite of each cake, chewing slowly; weighing each texture, taste and sensation. After she tasted the last cake she set the fork down.

"Well?" Drew asked.

"They're all very delicious."

A smug grin touched his face.

"But nothing like the cake you made."

His smile fell. He stared at her amazed. "What?"

"Your cake isn't in this selection."

"You could tell that?"

She sat back with triumph. "Of course I could. You didn't make any of these, did you?"

Drew slowly shook his head stupefied.

"The staff from your bakery?"

He nodded.

"Clearly you're a good teacher. But this one," she pointed to the one nearest her, "is a little dry. While this is a little heavy."

He blinked. "You're amazing. A natural."

She raised her hands up in the air as if expecting applause. "I know." She let her hands fall to the table. "One of my massage teachers said I had heightened senses and that they would serve me well."

Drew rubbed his chin and said in a soft whisper. "I don't believe this. Can you, Stuart?"

"Stuart?"

He cleared his throat. "Sorry, didn't mean to say that aloud."

"Who's Stuart?"

Drew hesitated, looking uncomfortable then said with some reluctance, "My older brother. Sometimes I still talk to him although he's no longer with us. So no, I'm not crazy or delusional."

"I didn't say you were. Does Theo talk to him too?"

"No, just me," he said, letting his voice and gaze fall for a moment before he lifted them again. "Stuart would have been fascinated by someone like you."

Clarice stood, feeling the weight of Drew's acceptance of his brother's death and his sorrow. She nodded towards the box of teas. "Would he have tried one of those?"

"Probably."

"Then I would have liked him too." She looked up towards the ceiling. "You should tell your brother to live a little."

Drew frowned, also looking up. "Who are you talking to?"

"Stuart of course."

"He's not up there." Drew pointed to the seat next to hers. "He's sitting right there."

She sat on the chair. "Oh, then would he mind me sitting on his lap?"

"He might not, but I would."

Clarice turned to the chair. "Your brother has no sense of humor."

Drew took her arm and lifted her from the chair. "He says you're heavier than you look."

She playfully hit him in the arm, causing him to smile. "I'll get you for that." She began to leave the kitchen then turned to him and twisted his nipple hard.

Drew winced and grabbed his chest. "You've got a mean streak. Are you really that sensitive about your weight?" he asked, rubbing his chest.

"No, that's for pretending not to remember me. Now I'm going."

"First promise me not to touch a red velvet cake until I get the chance to make one for you."

Clarice grinned. "You want to be my first time?"

He folded his arms. "You're talking dirty again."

"I know. I can't help it." She turned to the chair. "Sorry Stuart, I'm corrupting your younger brother and I should know better. I really should stop."

Drew nodded, maintaining a straight face. "Yes, you should," he said then watched her leave the kitchen before he added, "Because I'm starting to like it," in a voice too low for her to hear.

Chapter Twelve

He hadn't been honest.

It wasn't the first time Drew hadn't told Clarice the truth. The first was when he told her he was old enough to drink, the second was about Jennifer. He'd now done four more sessions with her and still hadn't told her the truth about their breakup.

Drew inspected the cookie drops laid out on the baking sheets to be put in the oven for the morning crowd, making sure they were flat and not filled with air bubbles. The baker who came in from four a.m. to eight a.m. usually did a good job making sure the texture was smooth, but Drew always liked to make sure when he arrived at six a.m. before the shop opened at seven. The bakery was already filled with the scent of cinnamon rolls and muffins, which would soon take their place in baskets for customers to choose.

As Drew made his quick inspection of the rows of cookies, he wondered why he hadn't told Clarice he'd had a meeting with Jennifer soon after the fiasco at the bakery.

She'd come a few days after the incident with a peace offering and a smile.

"Let's go for a drive," he said, meeting her smile with a stoic expression.

"I thought we could get some forks and eat here."

"I'd rather drive."

Moments into the silent drive, past familiar side streets where they use to walk hand-in-hand, she said, "I can't tell you how sorry I am, Drew. I don't know what came over me."

He tapped his thumb against the steering wheel. "I don't think we can see each other anymore."

"Don't say that."

"It's the truth."

"You just need some space," she said with a resigned sigh. "That's fine. I'll give it to you."

"You know how much I'm struggling to keep the bakery profitable. You could have slapped me, hit me, kicked me. Done anything to *me*," he said, hitting his chest with his fist. "But instead you attacked my very livelihood. Not just mine but all the people I employ."

"Drew—"

"And you did it publicly. Why didn't you come into the room that night? Face me then and there? Why did you wait until the next day?"

"I was so mad. I told you I couldn't bear to see you with another woman. I wasn't thinking. I heard what you were saying and turned away. I just couldn't believe it. All night I kept thinking of how I wanted to hurt you as much as you'd hurt me." She lightly rested her hand on his arm and softened her voice. "I told you I was sorry. How many ways can I say it until you believe me?"

He sighed. "I believe you, but that doesn't change anything."

"Why not? Tell me what you want me to do."

"There's nothing for you to do. There's nothing for
either of us to do."

"What happened the other day—"

"It's not just that. It's other things."

"What?"

He shook his head. "It doesn't matter. It's not working
between us."

She threw up her hands in exasperation. "I'll pay for the
cake. I'll pay for whatever you want. Give the staff a bonus.
I'm sorry I overreacted. I didn't mean it. You have to look
at things from my side."

"I do and I know you're getting tired of waiting. I can't
promise I'm the one for you."

"After a couple of years you'll see if this bakery
thing—"

"That's it. It's not a thing. If this doesn't work out I
can't pretend that I won't try again."

"But you promised."

He turned the car and headed back towards the bakery.
"I know. That's why I'm telling you now. I don't think I can
keep my promise. I'm not going to keep you waiting for me
to become the man you want to marry."

"We've gone through too much for us to give up now. I
was there for you when—"

"I know," he said in a tense voice. "I'll never forget that. I needed you then and you were there for me."

"But you don't need me now?" she said bitterly.

She knew how to make him feel guilty. To make him feel that he'd used her, but he hadn't. She'd been a glimmer of light in a very dark period of his life. She'd helped him through the pain of losing Stuart and taking care of Theo. She made every day worth living, but he didn't need that anymore.

If he hadn't been so desperate he would have seen the signs earlier that they weren't a good match. That she'd fallen in love with someone else—a man who would do or say anything to keep her by his side so he wouldn't be alone. After nearly two years together he realized that man was gone. "I don't think we have what it takes to last in the long run."

Jennifer fell silent for a long moment then said, "Promise me you won't see her."

"See who?"

"That woman. Clarice Yates. Tell me you won't see her again then I'll believe you weren't doing anything that night."

Drew gripped the steering wheel, his feelings of guilt melting like ice cream in an oven. "I'll see who I want to."

"Then I was right. You are seeing her behind my back. All those late nights you've been canceling on me where because of her."

He had canceled a lot more dates with her recently, but because of his back spasms and aching joints after working long days. He hadn't wanted to share his health concerns with her knowing she'd encourage him to give up what he loved. "No, I wasn't. I was—"

"I looked her up. I found out that she's not a massage therapist. She's an accountant. Just to give you the benefit of the doubt, when I spoke to someone at her office, I asked if she did massage on the side. The person talked to me as if I were crazy. You lied to me."

Drew rubbed his forehead and sighed. "I didn't lie. She's keeping it a secret. She's using me as practice." He parked the car at the side of the building and got out.

"You expect me to believe that?" Jennifer shouted as she exited the car.

He marched towards the bakery. "Okay, fine. I'm caught. I was with her last night. I couldn't help myself."

"And you want to leave me to be with her?"

"No. I want to leave you to be with someone who believes me when I tell them the truth the first time." He walked into the bakery and headed to the back.

Jennifer followed close behind. "Wait? What are you trying to say? Were you with her or not?"

Drew walked into his office and closed the door in her face.

Since then Jennifer hadn't stopped calling, texting and leaving him messages. Some, angry drunk tirades, others tearful admissions; others bossy demands and some sweet appeals. He ignored them all and hoped she'd soon get the point that they were finished and go away and find the rich man who would make her happy.

But that hope seemed to be further in the future when she stopped trying to reach him and instead tried to get to him through his nephew.

"Jennifer came by the school," Theo told him as he stacked the dinner plates in the dishwasher.

"Hmm."

"She told me that she wants you to call her. Are you fighting?"

Drew sighed. "We're no longer seeing each other." He pointed at his nephew. "And wipe that grin off your face."

"You mean you're not going to marry her?"

"No. And I told you to stop grinning."

He covered his mouth. "Sorry."

"She was good to us and I liked her," he said feeling the need to defend her, although he felt just as relieved as his nephew. "Remember when she came over with soup when we both had the cold? How she treated you to Wally World for your birthday?"

"Yes." He chewed his lip. "Are you sad?"

"A little."

Theo closed the dishwasher. "Will you miss her?"

"A little."

He hesitated, then walked to one of the boxes of herbal teas Drew still had sitting on the counter. He'd taken them out of their gift box and stacked them two by two. "Is it because of me?" he asked in a small voice.

"What?"

He lifted one of the boxes. "That you're not seeing her anymore."

"No." He playfully rubbed Theo's head. "Don't give yourself so much credit."

He nodded turning the box over in his hand. "Is Ms. Yates married?"

Drew took the box from him and set it back in its place. "No, but that has nothing to do with us."

He took another box. "I like her."

"I know," Drew said, taking the second box from him. "You told me."

"She doesn't know you don't like herbal teas so it's not fair to hate her 'cause of it."

He put the box back and straightened it, wishing his nephew would change the subject. "I don't hate her."

"Then how come you sound angry?"

"I'm not angry."

"And why are you keeping boxes you don't even like?"

He angrily knocked one of the carefully stacked boxes off of the counter with a flick of his wrist. "I don't know," he said, still unable to figure out his behavior.

Theo picked the box up off the ground. "Ms. Gladys likes—"

"Nobody is to touch these teas." He held up a hand when Theo started to protest. "I don't hate Ms. Yates and I just like looking at the boxes that's all."

"Oh." Theo set the box down. "Sometimes I think she's here."

"Who?"

"Ms. Yates. When I sit on the couch, sometimes it smells like her."

"It's probably Jennifer's perfume."

Theo frowned. "Jennifer doesn't smell like Ms. Yates. I told you, she's buttercream and I thought I smelled her the other day."

"Hmm," Drew said, not wanting to tell his nephew about Clarice's evening visits. He always managed to get him in bed before she came.

He sighed. "I miss her."

"Miss Yates?" Drew said surprised.

"No, Lady."

Drew nodded in understanding. Bran Muffin had come to collect her a few days ago. "You could ask him. I'll be with you if you do."

"I told you I'm scared of her and he is too."

"I'll be right there with you. If you don't ask, you'll never know if you can keep her."

He nodded, his shoulders sagging.

Drew affectionately tugged on Theo's superhero T-shirt. "Hey what's the expression for? I'm the one who broke up with my girlfriend. You know that Lady will be around again soon. You're supposed to tell me that you hope I find someone else."

"I hope you find somebody else." He walked to the door then added, "Who's not like Jennifer," before he dashed out the door.

Drew shook his head then turned on the dishwasher. His nephew didn't have to worry. He planned to be single for a while. He didn't think there would be another woman who would be as patient with him as Jennifer had been. And he doubted he could find someone who would understand his obligation to his family and his passion and drive. It was unfair to involve someone in his life when it wasn't yet stable.

Drew thought of the stack of teas and the taste of buttercream as he put a tray of cookies in the oven. He knew why he hadn't told Clarice that he'd broken up with Jennifer. He wasn't ready to admit he was free to pursue other flavors and he'd already found one that was just right.

Chapter Thirteen

"Oh, I forgot to tell you. Bob had the strangest call a couple days ago," Lois told Clarice as they finished their lunch in the tiny break room, that was beginning to smell more and more like the grilled trout salad Clarice had begged her mother not to bring to the office.

"Who?" Clarice said, hoping her clothes wouldn't smell like fish when she met with her next client.

"Some woman called asking about whether you do massage." She laughed. "Isn't that hilarious?"

Clarice swallowed. Her turkey sandwich becoming a lump in her throat. "Really?"

"Yes, he said she sounded adamant, but he told her that she had the wrong place. But she was still insistent it was you. Even called you by name. Isn't that strange?"

"Yes, very." Clarice set her sandwich down and wiped crumbs from her fingers. "Did she say anything more?"

"Nothing he could understand. Just that you…" She started to laugh. "…were in the back room…" She laughed harder. "Of some place with her boyfriend." She doubled over in laughter, slapping her lap. "*You* of all people. Isn't that hilarious?"

Clarice plastered on a smile. "A riot."

Lois wiped tears from her eyes. "We both had a good laugh about it. She clearly got you confused with someone else and it took Bob some time to convince her otherwise."

"Hmmm."

"I'm going to the movies tonight. Want to come?"

"I can't."

Lois frowned. "That's the third time."

"The third time what?"

"That's the third time I've asked you to do something and you've said you can't make it."

Clarice took a baby carrot and swirled it in her ranch dip. "You're keeping score?"

"It's just that it's rare for you to be so busy. What are you doing?"

She bit the carrot, and chewed slowly as her mind raced for an explanation. "A new hobby."

"What is it?"

"Cooking."

"You don't cook."

She nodded. "Exactly. I thought I should start."

"Why?"

Clarice finished the carrot and grabbed another one. *Good question.* "Because I'm curious. It's always nice to learn a new skill."

"What have you made so far?"

"Umm…cupcakes."

Lois waved her fork. "That's not cooking. That's bak-ing."

"Right. Right. That's what I meant. Baking."

"That's a dangerous hobby."

"Why?"

Her gaze swept Clarice's form. "Because it's fattening."

"Not if you have great willpower," Clarice said, thinking of Drew's tight abs and clearly defined pecs. She needed willpower too, to make sure her fingers didn't linger longer on his body than they needed to. She needed the willpower not to imagine conducting a taste test of cheesecake along the length of his torso without the use of a fork. She'd just use her tongue to…

"Maybe I should join."

"It's not a course," Clarice said quickly, shoving her fantasy to the back of her mind where it belonged. "It's something I'm doing online."

"Then we could do it together."

"I like learning on my own."

"Why? We always do things together."

That was true. Since the wedding disaster, she'd always made sure to be available for her mother. Especially in the early days when she feared her mother's depression would cause her mother to consider taking her own life. "Because I wanted to surprise you. I'm working on some recipes and they haven't turned out good yet."

"Do you like the instructor?"

The thought of Drew in his white chef's jacket came to mind, his warm hands over hers as he stood behind her, his hard chest against her back, showing her how to use a pastry bag to create swirls on a layered coconut cake. "Hmm."

"When will you finish this course?"

Clarice picked up her sandwich resisting the urge to fan herself. "Soon."

"Good. I expect you to bake me something delicious."

Chapter Fourteen

D elicious was the word that lingered in her mind days later as she kneaded Drew's hands. Although they were large, rough with scratches and cuts, they still managed to fascinate her by their ability to create mouthwatering masterpieces.

"I know you're going to bite my head off, but I'll say it anyway," Clarice said, keeping her voice as businesslike as possible. "You can't keep this schedule up. Aside from the fact that I think you should get a second opinion about the AS, even a healthy man will be run into the ground by all you're taking on. Long hours and lack of sleep will catch up with you." After several weeks they'd gotten into a rhythm of Drew telling her about the prior days' events.

"How did your skills test go?"

"We're not talking about me right now."

"We'll talk about me later," Drew said. "Wasn't your skills test this month?"

You remember that? I didn't think you were listening. "I decided not to take it."

"Why?"

That was the same question Luisa had asked her and Clarice hadn't had a good reason then either. But as Clarice gradually made her way down his arm the reason came to her. Massage was no longer the most important thing to her. She no longer just focused on his body—the deltoid, triceps branchii or pectoralis major—to practice her skills. She focused on the man. He was not some nameless and faceless chart of human muscle; she couldn't look at him with the distant interest of a clinician.

She saw him only as Drew and when she touched him it was personal. She didn't have the feelings a therapist should. And as much as she knew that what she felt was wrong, unethical, improper, she wanted to keep practicing so that she could continue to see him.

Twice a week she woke up, before the alarm, looking forward to the evening she'd get to spend with him. Time she knew wouldn't last forever, but time she didn't want to let go. She made her way down his other arm, his skin slick and warm under her fingers. "Just try to think about pulling back your schedule," she said, keeping her voice neutral though her feelings were not.

Drew sighed. Clarice knew he was disappointed she hadn't given him an answer, but didn't care. She'd never reveal her feelings to him. "You can make minor changes, right?" she said.

"I have to do it to keep the business running," he said. "I'm lucky to be busy and can't afford to turn anyone away."

Something about his business at the bakery didn't sit right with her, just as his AS diagnosis still made her question whether it was true or not. From the look of things, his business was booming. It received great publicity, was always full of customers, both new and returning and, through the spring and summer, did many catered events. Money had to be leaking from somewhere for him to have to keep up such an exhaustive schedule.

Clarice ended the session and wiped her hands. "Do you trust me?"

Drew slipped on his jeans. "Depends."

"Do you trust me to look at your books?"

He thought for a moment. "That's Gerry's territory, but I don't think he'd mind. I don't think there's much you can do." He grabbed a T-shirt and put it on. "He's been giving me ideas and they just haven't been panning out. I may have to face the fact that I'm no good at what I do."

Clarice rested a hand on her hip, her tone serious. "Your food is delicious and you know it."

His face split into a wide grin, his brown gaze bright with humor. "Yes, I know. I just like hearing you say it. By the way, I made you something."

"Really?"

"Yes. It's in the fridge on the third shelf. It's in a little white box."

Clarice eagerly disappeared into the kitchen and came out a few seconds later confused. She held up the box. "Is this it?"

He nodded.

She lifted the lid. "But it's empty."

Drew snatched the box from her, stunned. "What?" He looked inside and swore. "I don't believe this." He glanced up at her. "Don't look at me like that. I'm not angry at you." He squashed the box between his palms, flattening it like a pancake. "But I am angry."

"What was it supposed to be?"

He held up his forefinger. "Wait a minute. I'm thinking. Who was here last?" He folded his arms.

"While you figure that, out I'm going to use the bathroom before I leave."

Clarice went to the bathroom wondering what sweet treat he'd made for her. Unfortunately, someone had gotten to it first and it wasn't Theo or Drew would have suspected him right away. Jennifer maybe? He hadn't talked about her since the cake incident even when she hinted at how things were, but he liked to keep that part of his life private.

Clarice dried her hands then saw a red cloth bag, lying on its side at the bottom of the sink. It had a white medical logo on it and the name "Reinhart" stamped across it. She straightened the bag and heard the rattling sound of pills. She looked inside and saw three bottles. They didn't look like prescriptions. When she tried to read the name on one she couldn't understand the description. She replaced the bag. She'd ask Drew about them another time, she didn't want him to think she'd been snooping. Clarice left the bathroom then stopped when she saw a little head peeking around the corner.

"Hey, Theo. You couldn't sleep?"

He stared at her amazed and came into the hallway. "Ms. Yates, what are you doing here? Are you having a sleeping over like Uncle did with Jennifer?"

Clarice couldn't stop a laugh, feeling both amusement at Theo's innocence and a twinge of pain that Drew wasn't free. "No, I'm just helping your uncle."

Theo grabbed her hand and pulled her into his bedroom. "Could you help me too?"

She sat on the bed, her gaze sweeping over the light grey walls, and landing on a picture of Theo, Drew and another smiling man, Clarice guessed to be Stuart, sitting on Theo's dresser next to an action figure. "I don't know. What is it?"

"I want a dog," Theo said then sat beside her and commenced to tell her about Lady and the two neighbors. "So what should I do? The woman in 2B scares me."

"Why do you think you would be a better owner than her?"

"Because I'm nice and Lady likes me."

"She likes me too and I'm a great owner and love her very much."

Theo blinked and stared at her.

"I'm pretending to be her," Clarice explained.

"Oh," he said, relaxing a little. "She's much scarier than you."

"I can be scarier."

He frantically waved his hands. "No. No don't."

"But I should be so you can practice." She stood. "Now pretend to knock on my door and ask for Lady. Ready?"

He shook his head.

"Yes, you are. You can do this. Go on."

Theo rubbed his hands together then pretended to knock. Clarice mimed opening a door and folded her arms looking annoyed. "If you're selling something I'm not interested."

He frowned. "But I'm not selling anything."

"I know," Clarice said with patience. "But when you knock on her door she might think you are. What would you say?"

He flexed his fingers and rocked back and forth on his heels. "I don't know."

"You say you want to talk about Lady."

"Okay, I want to talk about Lady."

Clarice changed her tone and expression to mimic the scary neighbor. "What about Lady?"

Theo stared at her for a long moment then hung his head. "I can't do it."

Clarice glanced at one of the action figures on his dresser. "What if Lady's in danger?"

His head snapped up. "What?"

"What if the only way you can save her is if you get this neighbor to let her go." She tugged on his Green Lantern pajamas. "You have to be her hero."

"Her hero?"

"Yes, what would you do? Just pretend. Stand up straight that's it. Now try again. What are you doing at my door?"

He took a deep breath. "I want to look after Lady. I know you are really busy and she likes to visit us. You could come by and see her so I wouldn't be taking her far, but I could look after her so you wouldn't have to worry."

Clarice rested a hand on his shoulder. "Very good. Do that."

"What if she says no?"

"At least you tried."

"What if she's mean to me?"

"I don't think she'll be that mean with your uncle standing next to you." Clarice squeezed his shoulder. "Remember Lady needs your help. Don't let her down." She turned to the door. "Now I'd better go before your uncle wonders where I've disappeared to."

"Are you going to come over again?"

Not to sleep over, unfortunately. "Yes."

He hesitated. "Sometimes Uncle is sad because he's all alone now."

"He's not alone. He has you and Jennifer."

"He doesn't have Jennifer anymore. They broke up."

"Oh, I'm sorry," Clarice said not knowing how to take the news. She said goodnight to Theo then slowly made her way down the hall. Drew was single again. But why had he kept it secret? Did they break up because of what happened? Did he sense her attraction and want to keep her at a distance? Maybe she was being selfish and should have ended her practice sessions weeks ago. Maybe she should end it now. She'd let herself imagine that they were closer than they were, but she'd been fooling herself.

Chapter Fifteen

ury nearly choked him.

Once Clarice had left the room, Drew had taken his anger out on the little box, which had once contained a tiny fresh fruit tart of kiwi slices, strawberries, blueberries and raspberries, which he'd carefully made, before throwing the box away. He'd really hoped to surprise her tonight and he knew who had stolen that pleasure from him.

He dialed Gladys' number.

"Do you know what time it is?" she demanded when she answered the phone.

"I know exactly what time it is," Drew said in a soft voice.

"Oh." Her tone turned wary. "Is something wrong?"

"How many times have I told you not to help yourself to food in my kitchen? I've made it clear the items you can touch."

"But I didn't—"

"I opened the box."

"I was going to tell you."

"When?"

"I thought I'd get enough time to replace it," she said in a rush. "I just took one little tiny taste but then it left a space so I thought to even it out by taking a little more and before I knew it, it was all gone. I'll pay you."

He ground his teeth. He was getting real tired of people offering him money when they annoyed him. But if she wanted to pay, he wouldn't stop her. "You're lucky it wasn't my red velvet."

"What?"

"Never mind. You owe me twenty-five."

"Cents?"

He didn't reply.

"You can't mean dollars!"

He still remained silent.

"Twenty-five dollars! It was just a little tart."

"I'm also charging you for pain and suffering. It was meant to be a gift. Bye." He cut off her protests by disconnecting the call.

Clarice nodded to his cell phone. "I couldn't help overhearing. You're not really going to charge twenty-five dollars, are you?"

"Yes, and I'm being generous." His frown increased when she smiled at him. "What's that expression for?"

"Just the thought that you made me something makes me happy, especially since…" Her smile dimmed; she turned. "I have to go."

He grabbed her arm and forced her to face him. "Especially since what?"

"It's nothing."

"Tell me."

She lowered her gaze. "You've made it clear that your private life is none of my business, but," she lifted her gaze, "why did you keep pretending you were still with Jennifer? Do I make you so uncomfortable that you have to lie—?"

He didn't let her to finish, covering her mouth with his in a way that left her breathless. When he drew away she stared at him stunned.

"I'm sorry," he said.

Clarice swallowed, her heart thundering. "Sorry that you kissed me?"

A quick grin came and went. "No, that I didn't tell you sooner. Don't ask me why. I don't know." He snaked an arm around her waist and pulled her close. When he spoke his voice was barely a whisper. "But I do know one thing. How much I want you." He kissed her again.

"What did you make for me?" she asked against his lips.

"A fruit tart."

"I think you taste better."

He pressed his lips against her throat, his breath warm against her skin when he spoke. "We'll conduct a taste test later."

"It may take a while. I want to be very thorough."

"And I'm very patient."

Clarice placed her hand on his chest. "But we can't do this."

"Why not?" he asked, dropping a kiss behind her ear.

"I'm supposed to be your massage therapist."

"It was only practice." He pressed her body closer to his, his voice dropping into huskiness. "Can't a massage therapist practice on her boyfriend?"

"I'll have to think about the ethics of that," she teased already knowing what her decision would be.

Drew kissed her once more before letting her go. "Don't think too long. Or I'll make up your mind for you."

"I'd better go."

His heated gaze held her still. "Even if I want you to stay?"

"We both have to work tomorrow," she said, though she didn't move.

He drew her to him once more. "I don't mind staying up all night."

"That's why you'll hurt the next day."

"That's all right," he said holding her close. "You know how to make me feel better."

Clarice slid out of his grasp, resisting the temptation to stay. "Another time. I can't be distracted right now. I want you to schedule a meeting with Gerry so I can look at your books and see what's going on."

Chapter Sixteen

Gerry had something to hide. Clarice could sense it the moment she met him at the bakery once it had closed for the day. She watched his mustache twitch when Drew introduced her and told him why they were there. Although the scent of sugar and fresh bread still hung in the air, something about Gerry stank.

"What, you don't trust me?" Gerry laughed, although the sound didn't ring true.

"That's not it," Drew said. "She just—"

"Oh, I get it." He winked. "Trying to impress the new girlfriend, huh? Don't worry," he said to Clarice with a wide grin. "I look after Drew and the business as if it were my own."

"She's an accountant."

Gerry's smile dimmed. "We already have an accountant. Someone I've used for years."

Clarice folded her arms and continued to watch Gerry. His defensive posture told her all she needed to know. "Drew, could I speak to Gerry alone for a minute?"

He hesitated then stood and motioned her to join him. "We'll be back in a second," he said to Gerry before he led Clarice far enough away so that Gerry couldn't overhear. "I didn't tell him you were my girlfriend because he and Jennifer didn't always see eye to eye and—"

"That's fine. I understand why you didn't."

"Then why do you want to talk to him alone?"

"It's a money thing. I want to save his pride in case he made a mistake. I don't think he'll feel comfortable talking to me with you there."

"Gerry's not that kind of guy. When I was a teenager, he'd let me tell him when something wasn't working right."

"Money can be a touchier subject. You said you trusted me, right? Or do you only trust me with your body?"

The beginning of a smile tipped the corners of his mouth. "Okay, you win. I'll be in the back."

Clarice returned to her seat and pinned Gerry with a look.

"What are you hiding?"

"Who says I'm hiding anything?"

She pointed. "Your tense shoulders, the flicker in your right pinkie."

"It's a nervous twitch."

"And your unwillingness to let me see what you've been up to. We didn't even need to meet here; you could have sent the material to me online."

"Drew trusts me."

"And he probably shouldn't. He's working like a dog for revenue he's not seeing. Where is it going?"

Gerry pushed his chair back and stood. "I don't have to discuss this with you."

"No, I'm talking to you out of courtesy, but do you really want Drew to see what you've done?"

"I haven't done anything." He turned to the door. "Tell Drew I'll see him later."

"You really hate him, don't you?"

He spun around, his eyes black. "You don't know anything."

"I see the way you look at Drew and it isn't with affection. You may be able to fool others, but you can't fool me. I'm the queen of pretence. I can smile at a man I want to break in two."

Gerry took a menacing step towards her. "I don't know who you are, but you'd better not mess with me."

"Why not?" Drew asked.

Gerry looked up; Clarice spun around.

Drew walked towards them. His gait was casual, but his tone was not. "Why shouldn't she mess with you?"

Gerry rubbed his forehead. "I was feeling threatened. I don't know what I was saying."

"Yes, you did," Clarice said.

"Don't listen to her, Drew." Gerry held out his hands and smiled. "Come on you know me. You've known me since you were fourteen. We have history. You'd have thought I'd have gained your trust by now."

"He's hiding something."

     Dara Girard

"No, I'm not."

"Then why won't you let me see the books? Why is the bakery still just squeaking by? Why—?"

"Because he wasn't supposed to win," Gerry shouted, sinking into one of the chairs. "He wasn't supposed to take it from me." He covered his face.

Clarice blinked. "What?"

"The bakery was something I'd always dreamed about." He let his hands fall to the table. "I slaved away in a cubicle for thirty years and then retired and opened up this place right when the market was heading down. I didn't think I'd make it. I didn't expect to." He stared up at Drew with pain and envy in his eyes. "I offered you that bet because I…never in a million years thought you would succeed. But when you came back waving that check it was like a knife in my heart."

"But we were partners," Drew said.

"I thought that would help me deal with my envy, but it didn't. You kept getting better and better. Showing me all my flaws and weaknesses. Some kid who never had to work at a job that undervalued him for decades. You just walked in and flourished. At first I didn't want you getting too cocky. I made it a little tough so that you'd develop grit. I've seen what easy success can do. It can ruin a man. I didn't want to see that happen to you."

Clarice stood and kicked Gerry's chair, startling the older man. "You expect us to believe that garbage? What about after Drew became the sole owner?"

"Clarice," Drew said.

She kicked Gerry's chair again. "You're a petty, vengeful man and you were only thinking of yourself." She kicked his chair a third time.

Drew pulled her away. "Stop that."

"He's lucky I'm not kicking him." She glared at Gerry. "Do you know what you've been doing to him? Do you know that he might have—"

"Clarice," Drew warned.

"Gotten sick because of you?" she said, wishing she could throw the possible AS diagnosis in Gerry's face to make him feel guilty. She wanted to tell him about the back spasms and painful joints, the times Drew had made it through the day with tears right behind his eyes. How he had suffered to keep his staff's spirits up and pretend that everything was fine.

Gerry looked at Drew, a plea in his voice. "I'll find a way to get the money back."

Drew hung his head. "How many years?"

"I promise you."

Drew looked at him with sadness. "How long?"

"Long enough."

"You hated me that much?"

"I told you, I did it for you. Not because I hated you."

"Keep telling yourself that," Clarice said with a sneer.

Gerry's pleading tone swiftly disappeared; he stared at Clarice with disdain. "What did you say your name was again? Yates?"

"Yes, Clarice Yates."

"Why does that name sound familiar?"

"You should go now," Drew said.

Gerry pointed at her and narrowed his eyes. "Yates-Siggins. Does that mean anything to you?"

Clarice stiffened at the memory of the ruined wedding day. "Yes."

Drew shook his head. "Not now Gerry."

His gaze darted between them then his voice turned lewd. "Is this the one you spoke to? Is there something you're not telling me? You were young then, did you make any promises you got paid for that—"

"Say another word and I'll press charges."

Gerry flashed him a glare then stormed out.

Clarice watched him leave. "What was that about?"

"Never mind. What should we do first?"

"Right now you're going to change access to all your accounts."

The books were in a mess. Gerry had complete access to the banking account and was responsible for paying vendors. As a result he had added several bogus accounts and made payments to himself. He also inflated the costs of some of the ingredients and suppliers. This kept the expenses high and the profit low. Drew never thought to question the financial statements he received and had completely depended on Gerry.

Clarice spent a week uncovering and cleaning up the fraud, but she knew that would be just a minor fix. She could easily make the company appear more profitable but cash was still an issue. Plus, she still needed to find a way to make Delites Bakery more revenue with less effort, especially on Drew's side. He couldn't maintain his present pace. Instead of being the go-to cake decorator for every event imaginable, he needed to be more exclusive.

Then he could charge more for less. That meant getting him a higher paying clientele for the cakes.

At first Drew was dubious of the idea.

"What if I lose customers?"

"You will. That's the point. People who want quick, cheap and cheerful cakes can go somewhere else. If they want extraordinary designs they can't get elsewhere they'll come to you and pay for the privilege. You'll see, the more exclusive you are, the more booked you'll be and the less stressed out."

She hired Carl to take new pictures of the food—salted caramel squares, chocolate almond bars, bread pudding—and had another friend redesign the website with a big 'by appointment only' sign for the cake selection. Then she called her father and said, "I need a favor."

Chapter Seventeen

Theo looked like he'd won the moon as he held Lady in his arms and carried her to their apartment.

"Good job, buddy," Drew said. "I knew you could do it."

"She wasn't as scary as I thought."

"I told you."

"Ms. Yates helped."

Drew paused surprised. "When did you speak to her?"

Theo shrugged, adjusting Lady in his arms. "Just one night when she was helping you."

Drew started walking again. "A night when you should have been in bed?"

"I couldn't sleep. I didn't bother her, honest. She said she wanted to help."

Drew nodded. He was too happy for Theo to be upset with him. He actually hadn't expected it to happen so simply. His nephew had gotten lucky. Bran Muffin quickly said he could have the dog, sharing how much he'd loved having a dog as a kid and how much he felt his ex was spoiling Lady and when Theo knocked on Lemon Ripple's door and gave his little speech, she burst into tears.

"I don't believe it," she said.

"I'll take good care of her," Theo said, casting a nervous glance at his uncle.

"I know. That's why it's so perfect. I was planning to leave because I can't stand being around that man any more, but my new place doesn't allow pets and I didn't know what I was going to do. You came just in time. Now I know my baby is in good hands."

She then loaded Drew with all of Lady's things, kissed Theo on the forehead and said goodbye to Lady.

"I can't wait 'til Ms. Yates meets her," Theo said, setting Lady on the ground once they reached their apartment.

Drew unlocked the door. "I think she'll like her."

"Why can't Ms. Yates spend the night?"

Drew turned sharply to him. "What?"

"You used to let Jennifer spend the night all the time."

To his annoyance, Drew felt heat rise in his face. "S-she's busy. She works a lot."

"But it's the weekend."

"She's not ready to sleep over yet."

His face brightened. "Does that mean you like her?"

Drew couldn't help a smile. "Yes, I like her very much."

"I knew it. I knew it. Buttercream goes with anything. You've gotta make her the cupcakes Uncle."

"Which ones?" Drew said with a laughed pleased by his nephew's excitement.

"The ones where we add cocoa and mash up M&Ms and stuff."

"And add them to the buttercream frosting?" Drew said.

"Yeah, yeah that." Theo suddenly frowned. "But she might not like M&Ms. Remember when I added M&Ms to your oatmeal peanut butter cookies and gave them to Jennifer, she didn't like it because she said it was too lumpy. And what if Ms. Yates is on a diet? Remember when Jennifer was on a diet and—"

"Ms. Yates isn't on a diet."

"So we can make the cupcakes? And can she come over for dinner? And can I start calling her Aunty Clarice?"

Drew held up his hands. "Whoa, whoa slow down. We're just friends now."

"But I think she's lucky. She helped you when you hurt your back, and she helped me get Lady and you broke up with Jennifer."

Drew lifted a brow. "Breaking up with Jennifer had nothing to do with Clarice."

"Can I call her now? Pleaseeeee." Theo held his hands together. "I just want to tell her my news. And I won't talk long. I promise."

Drew handed him his cell phone. "Go on then."

Theo scrolled through his address book. "I can't find her."

Drew grabbed the phone, remembering he'd put Clarice under the name 'Red Velvet'. He hit it then handed it back to his nephew. "There you go," he said before he grabbed

Lady's items and took them to the kitchen. He was happy Theo liked Clarice, but didn't want him getting too attached to her. He'd been more cautious when introducing him to Jennifer, but he hadn't had that chance with Clarice. He hoped that Theo didn't end up hurt.

Drew made a quick victory snack for them of pretzels and grapes (Theo liked to organize the pretzel sticks and green grapes into a tree. The sticks acting as the trunk and roots and the grapes as the leaves) and returned to the living room surprised to see his nephew still on the phone. As he got closer he realized he was the topic of conversation.

"Yes, and he likes orange marmalade, but he doesn't like hot sauce and don't—" Theo paused when he saw Drew standing in front of him. "I'd better go. Bye."

Drew set the plate down. "I thought you said you wouldn't talk long."

"I didn't."

Drew gestured to the hall. "Go wash your hands." Theo ran down the hall, moments later Drew heard the sound of rushing water, he was about to tell his nephew not to waste it when his phone rang. He glanced down and saw Clarice's number.

"I'm sorry about that," he said.

She laughed. "He's a fountain of information about you."

"All lies."

"Oh, so you *do* leave whiskers in the sink after you shave?"

Drew briefly closed his eyes, feeling his face burn. "He told you that?" He opened his eyes and saw Theo standing in the hallway. He motioned for him to come closer and sit down.

"He wanted me to know that you're very clean," Clarice said. "He said Jennifer thought it was very important."

Drew kept his gaze on his nephew. "There are probably a few things I should tell you about him."

Theo quickly shook his head and frantically waved his hands.

Clarice laughed. "I'm sure I'll find out on my own, but I didn't call you about him."

"What is it?" Drew asked, watching Theo arrange the food on the plate.

"I've just sent you information about a possible job. Let me know what you think."

"Okay, hold on." He checked the message on his phone and blinked unable to believe his eyes. It was a job for a four tier vanilla champagne cake for a wedding in Port Antonio, Jamaica. "You've got to be kidding me."

"You don't think you can do it?"

"They want to pay me this much for one of my cakes?"

"I know," Clarice said disappointed. "I tried to make the profit margin a little wider, but she was adamant since she'll be covering your travel expenses and accommodation."

"What?"

"This will be worth it," Clarice said misinterpreting his tone of surprise. "This woman is a socially connected woman of influence. I told her about the castle cake and let her see pictures and she's willing to try you out. If you get in her good graces your name will spread. And—"

"You don't have to convince me. I'll do it."

"Great. My plan is to eventually let you pick your price and schedule. That way you won't have to work as much, get more sleep and you can be kind to your joints."

"I want you to come with me. If I can pull off something this big, I'll need a massage later."

"Drew."

"Just this once. It'd be nice to know you have my back."

"Okay," she said with some reluctance. "But just this once."

"Thank you." Drew hung up then pumped the air.

Theo grinned. "Was that Ms. Clarice?"

Drew schooled his features, knowing he'd been grinning like a kid at Christmas. "Yes. Ms. Gladys will be looking after you for a couple of days. Will you be okay, or would you like me to ask your—"

"No, no Ms. Gladys is fine. Where are you going? Can't I come too?"

"No, not this time. It's for a big cake job Clarice got for me."

Theo popped a grape in his mouth. "Told you she was lucky."

Drew took a pretzel. It certainly looked like it. "First, let's see if I can pull this off."

Chapter Eighteen

A Caribbean sea breeze rode on the scent of hibiscus as the sun melted into the horizon in a blaze of color, but Drew barely noticed it as he stood on the balcony of the hotel room where he was staying. Everything had gone perfectly so far. Clarice had made sure he had total reign of a section of the kitchen he needed at the hotel and had all the tools and ingredients ready. The cake had been one of his best, he'd even helped cut it when the catering crew didn't have the correct utensils, but he knew it was just the beginning.

"Okay," Clarice said. "The massage table is all ready for you maestro."

"Come out here with me for a second." When she joined him, Drew clasped her hand in his as he continued to stare out at the setting sun. "I wouldn't be here if it weren't for you."

"You did all the hard work."

He shook his head. "No, I mean it. If you hadn't given me that check all those years ago, I wouldn't own Delites."

"I don't understand."

"When Gerry was going on about the Yates-Siggins wedding…he was referring to a bet. He didn't think I could get you to pay the full amount."

"Oh," Clarice said with new understanding. "That's why he was so upset?"

Drew nodded.

"He's still a jerk."

"He wasn't always, or if he was," Drew continued when Clarice opened her mouth to argue, "I didn't see it at the time."

"That's not your fault."

"I looked up to him. I thought…I thought we were friends." He rested their joined hands on the railing. "Anyway, thanks for everything."

She took a step back and pulled him towards the sliding glass door. "Come on, let me do some massage."

"I don't want a massage." He swept her into his arms. "I want you." He walked to the bed. "I think I'll always want you," he said before he kissed her.

She wrapped her arms around his neck and kissed him back. "Why want what you already have?"

"Part of me can't believe this is real."

"You were a success."

"I'm not talking about the cake, I'm talking about us." He laid her on the bed.

"We're both very real." She slowly began to take off her blouse then stopped when he gritted his teeth and swore. "What is it?"

He squeezed his eyes closed. "My leg."

She touched his leg, the muscle was as hard as a stone. She silently scolded herself. Between the flight, the baking, and the party he had overexerted himself. She should have known that his body wouldn't be able to take more, no matter how pleasurable. She switched from girlfriend mode to therapist. "Okay, okay," she said in a gentle voice. "You know what to do."

He swore again with more feeling, as he fell back on the bed. "I'm tired, Clarice," he said in a weary voice of despair. "I'm so tired of this. I'm tired of the pain."

"I know," she said in a tender tone, kneading his muscle. Slowly she got the muscle to relax. "We still need to figure out what's going on. Who's your doctor?"

"Elizabeth Reinhart. She gave me some pills but they didn't work."

Reinhart. Reinhart. Why did that name sound familiar? "Okay, when we get back I want to see her full diagnosis and get a second opinion. Right now I'll draw you an Epsom salt bath."

"That's not how I wanted to spend the evening. Damn, I'm already living like an old man."

"Would you still think that if I said I planned to join you?"

His eyes met hers. "Don't tease me."

"I'm not."

He swung his legs over the side of the bed and limped towards the bathroom. "I'll draw it myself."

Clarice laughed and jumped in front of him. "Slow down or you'll hurt yourself." She turned and walked into the bathroom where a large claw tub sat. "Let me go start the hot water."

"I want to watch."

"Won't that be boring? At least wait until the bath is ready."

"Watching you is never boring," he said in a silky tone.

Clarice never imagined that drawing a bath could feel so sensual. For the first time she became aware of the rush of the water through the faucet, the rise of steam in the air, the scent of lavender from the purple crystals she poured into the water, the heat in the room, the feel of his gaze, the sensation of water running through her fingers.

"Is it ready yet?" Drew whispered in her ear, causing her to jump.

"Yes," she said a little breathless. "I didn't know you were so close."

"I like watching you up close," he said, his finger sliding down her steamed-soaked cheek.

She turned off the faucet. The sudden quiet making her even more aware of him, of what they were about to do. "You should get in first while it's hot."

He stripped down, slid into the bath then looked up at her. "Your turn. Wait." His voice cracked in outrage when she turned to the door. "Where are you going? I thought you said you weren't teasing me."

"I'm not," she said in a rush before he got out of the bathtub. "I'll be right back." She dashed out the door then closed it and searched the room for a robe. She hadn't anticipated a night like this so she hadn't been prepared. She'd been so focused on Drew's success as a baker and then later helping him as a massage therapist that she hadn't even anticipated that their time together might turn romantic.

She quickly took off her top and jeans then stared down with despair (and slight disgust) at her bra and panties—two items that looked like she'd retrieved them at a bargain sale at a senior's bazaar, which wasn't too far from the truth. The bra was a boring tan better suited for a highly religious woman three times her age and her underwear was so large it could have covered a man's head. They both knew she was older than him, but she didn't want to remind him of the fact.

Clarice removed them then grabbed his robe and wrapped it around her, stuffing the bra and panties in the pockets.

She returned to the bathroom.

Drew glared at her. "I was just about to come get you."

"I told you I would come back. You need to learn to trust me," she said, letting the robe slide off her body before she slipped into the water and into his arms. And when their bodies touched, she felt transported; her lips seeking sanctuary against his. At last she was close to him in ways she'd dreamt about. She'd told no one about him yet, he was a sweet secret she treasured and with her mouth, hands and body she told him so.

And Drew held her close as if in one moment she'd disappear. After losing Stuart he'd never thought he could feel this much pleasure again. Only a few moments ago his body had betrayed him, but she'd erased that memory as though he were a child awakened from a nightmare.

He still felt like he was living between two worlds—the nightmare of losing Stuart, of Gerry's betrayal, of his body failing him and the dream of spending time with someone who understood him, who wanted to help him achieve his heart's desire.

They stayed in each other's arms, Drew determined to count Clarice's every freckle, until the water got cold and the sun had disappeared.

Drew got out first and put on the robe before handing her a large towel.

"Let's order something," he began then stopped when he felt something in the pocket. He pulled it out. "What the—?"

Clarice reached for it. "That's mine."

He stepped back and held up the panties like a banner. "It can't be."

She reached for them again. "Just give it back."

Drew laughed. "These are big enough to cover the state of Texas." He stretched it to the side. "And New Mexico."

Clarice folded her arms. "Don't do that or it will lose its shape."

"What shape? What exactly are you trying to do? Cover your entire torso?"

She reached for his chest, but he quickly stepped back, covering his nipples. "Oh no. I'm not letting you do that to me again."

She held out her hand. "Then give them back to me or I'll make you wonder when I'll attack again."

He handed them to her. "We have to take you shopping."

"I didn't expect you to see them. Next time I'll be prepared." She reached into the pocket of the robe and grabbed her bra before she spun to the door.

Drew grabbed her around the waist, pulling her back to him. He rested his chin on her shoulder. "Don't be mad. I was just teasing. I don't care what you wear. As long as you let me take it off."

She wiggled out of his grasp and opened the bathroom door. "Let's go to bed."

He pushed past her. "I like the sound of that."

"You need to rest."

He sat down on the bed and frowned up at her. "That's just mean."

She pushed him back. "Come on. Lie down."

"What about a massage?"

"I'm too tired do to it. Now lie down."

"Only if you'll lie down with me."

"No."

"Why not? I won't do anything."

"Yes, you will."

A mischievous grin spread on his face. "Wise woman."

She pushed him back, but before he fell backward on the bed he wrapped his arms around her and took her with him.

"What are you doing?"

"Getting comfortable," he said, rolling to his side.

"Let go. At least let me get changed."

He sighed. "Just stay with me for a minute. Okay? I really am too tired to do anything else."

"I should say no."

He kissed the back of her neck. "And I should let go."

"But you won't?"

He shook his head.

"Why not?"

"Because you're my lucky charm. When I'm with you amazing things happen."

His words proved prophetic. Within weeks of the wedding in Jamaica, Drew's name spread and soon he had commissions from Montreal to Kingston. New York to Seattle. And was booked for the next two years. As much as possible, he wanted her to travel with him so they scheduled events so that Clarice could clear her calendar and tell her mother a lie (that she was attending a workshop, a conference, had a cold) and the brief reprieve would usually only be for two days but the thought of spending time with him was exciting and she loved seeing him at work.

In the summer, they scheduled a way for Theo to join them, although they knew once autumn came they'd have to leave him with Gladys so he could go to school. Clarice knew all their planning was for a future that hadn't happened yet, but still loved the thought.

Drew no longer had to worry about saving his business, but his health still worried her.

Chapter Nineteen

"Dr. Elizabeth Reinhart?" Luisa said in disbelief. "I can't believe that woman is still in practice." She and Clarice sat in Luisa's exquisitely designed office, the soft sound of chanting monks coming from the tiny speakers hidden in the room.

"That bad huh?" Clarice said, sipping her green tea.

"The worst. She's known for giving devastating diagnosis then charging her patients for pills that are supposed to help them. She was involved with several medical malpractice lawsuits."

Clarice snapped her fingers as she remembered the bag in Drew's bathroom with the medical logo and bottle of pills. "I knew that name sounded familiar. She's done a good job of burying her past. When I did a quick search online none of that came up."

"I'm not surprised," Luisa said in a grave tone. "She, or others, has put up enough glowing reports to squash the rest."

"So, Drew probably doesn't have AS," Clarice said to herself.

"I wouldn't trust anything Reinhart says. Let him get a second opinion."

"I will."

"What do you suspect is the problem?"

"Oh…I couldn't—"

"This is all hypothetical. I'm just asking you what you think is wrong."

"It's just a sense, but he may need a simple remedy."

"Then put that into action too. You may surprise yourself. You're more intuitive than you think. In the mean time make sure he never sees that woman again."

"Don't worry. I will."

Luisa clasped her hands together on the desk. "I was sort of hoping that you'd wanted to see me because you'd changed your mind. Is that still a possibility?"

"No, I'm fine doing what I do."

"Okay," Luisa said and she smiled, but the expression didn't reach her eyes.

Drew stared at Clarice, dubious. "A fraud?"

They stood in the kitchen where Clarice had put two bags of groceries on the table before she told him about her conversation with Luisa. The sound of Theo playing with Lady could be heard from the open screen door leading to the back, the room warm from the evening summer heat since Drew didn't like using the air conditioner at high levels.

But as Clarice looked at Drew's face she felt a distinct chill in the air. The news she'd given him hadn't made him happy. "Yes."

"You're sure."

"Yes, and I already have the name of someone you can see for a second opinion. Okay?"

He absently nodded. "You're absolutely sure about Dr. Reinhart?"

"Yes."

He rubbed the back of his neck. "That explains why the pills didn't work."

"How long did you take them?"

Drew ducked his head in the familiar fashion that made him look both fierce and vulnerable. Although the motion was familiar, Clarice still couldn't interpret what he was thinking. "Not long."

"That's good."

He folded his arms. "You must think I'm a real idiot."

"No," Clarice said surprised by the accusation. "Why would I think that?"

"Right away you knew Gerry was ripping me off and now you're telling me my doctor was doing the same." He shook his head. "No, worse."

"It could happen to anyone."

"Just some more than others, hmm?" he said in a cool tone. "Has something like this ever happened to you?"

Clarice thought for a moment. "Once when I was a kid—"

"So I guess wisdom comes with age, right?" he said, his dark gaze studying her with an intensity she'd never seen before.

Clarice cleared her throat, his sudden scrutiny made her uneasy. "What's that supposed to mean?" she asked because she didn't know what else to say, as the meaning of his words slowly sunk in, wounding her.

"Never mind."

She lifted her bags, wishing she hadn't told him. Did he have to remind her about their age difference? Did he think she was mothering him? "I'm sorry I pricked your pride. I thought I was dating a man not a teenager." She began to leave.

Drew grabbed her arm and spun her back to him. "No, wait. I'm sorry."

Her eyes blazed up at him. "Do you really think you're supposed to know everything about the world before you turn thirty?"

He lowered his gaze, chagrined. "It's not that. I'm sorry. Just…just ignore what I said."

"I was trying to help."

He lifted his gaze to hers, his eyes no longer hard, but pleading. "I know and I appreciate it." His jaw twitched. "It's just…"

"It's just what?" she pressed when he stopped, wanting to understand the plea in his eyes.

Drew started to speak, then Theo came bounding into the room with Lady. Drew took one of the bags from her. "What's all this then?"

"An experiment," Clarice said sorry she wouldn't be able to hear what he'd wanted to say. She set her other bag back on the table. "I'm hoping to alter your diet," she said then shared her idea.

"Are you serious?" Drew asked when she finished, picking up the avocado from the bag of groceries she had placed on the table.

Theo inspected the carton of tiny tomatoes while Lady daintily licked water from her bowl. "That means he doesn't like it," he said.

"No, that's not what I mean," Drew said.

"I know it sounds simple and I may be wrong," Clarice said, "but I think you may be lacking in potassium and or magnesium," She'd suspected that some of his muscle spasms could be related to an electrolyte imbalance.

Although he'd agreed to get a second opinion with a doctor she'd recommended, she'd wanted to try something new in the meantime and after seeing how often Drew missed main meals, she thought this could be a possible solution.

"I'm not a big vegetable man."

"And that might be the problem, but you can also try dried fruit, bananas, or cantaloupe."

"How much did you spend?"

"Doesn't matter. Of course you don't have to do this. I'd hate for you to think I was your mother."

Drew shot her a look.

Theo laughed. "Why would he think that? He already has a mother."

"Well, sometimes when someone is older than you are—"

"When are you planning on starting this experiment?" Drew cut in.

"Today. Theo, would you like to help me?"

He nodded.

"Drew, why don't you wait outside? You can suck on your thumb or something."

He didn't move, his eyes roaming over her figure, lingering on her chest then below her waist, before returning to her face. "I could think of a few other things I'd prefer to suck," he said in velvet tones.

Clarice blushed, imaging every freckle burning.

Theo frowned. "Like what? A popsicle?"

"Yes," Clarice said quickly. "That's what your uncle meant."

"But we don't have any more."

"Pity," Drew said, his gaze never leaving hers.

I'm sorry, Clarice mouthed over Theo's head, hoping he'd forgive her for teasing him, and let the topic drop. He nodded then rubbed the top of Theo's head and said, "Make me something good," before he left.

Together they made rainbow colored veggie kabob with, red tomatoes, orange carrots, yellow squash, green peppers and broccoli, and purple grapes. When Theo placed their creation in front of his uncle, with a hummus dip, he waited, anxious.

Drew took a bite then nodded. "Not bad."

Clarice high fived Theo. "Success!" she said, making him laugh.

But after all the dishes had been cleared and Clarice had gone home, Drew found Theo sitting in the living room looking glum as he absently stroked Lady.

He sat down beside him. "What is it?"

"I'm sad."

"Why?"

He lowered his head, his voice soft on the verge of tears. "Because I'm so happy."

Drew rested his arm around Theo's thin shoulders and sighed understanding the contradiction. He felt it too sometimes. "It's not a bad thing."

"If Dad—" He stopped and bit his lip.

Drew squeezed his arm. "It's okay to talk about him."

"I just wish Dad could be here too."

"I know. I wish the same thing."

He looked up at his uncle. "He'd like Lady and Clarice too."

"Yes, he would."

"Can Clarice come see him with us?"

Drew hesitated. In the early days he'd let Theo visit as much as he needed since he never wanted to break Theo's bond with his father while also facing the reality of what no longer was. But Drew wasn't ready to face that truth with Clarice. He missed his brother and sometimes he wondered if the ache would ever go away.

"It's okay," Theo said quickly, sensing his uncle's change in mood. "I didn't mean—"

"One day maybe, but not yet." *Maybe not ever.*

Chapter Twenty

"Business looks good," an older man with greying hair said, coming into the bakery shop, a rush of cold chill from the autumn breeze sweeping in with him.

Drew smiled at his weekly customer who he only knew as Murray. Murray had become a new regular over the past two months. While the big cake projects helped keep revenue high, it was the customers like Murray that Drew truly enjoyed. The ordinary people who liked to sweeten their day at the shop were one of the reasons at fourteen he knew what he wanted to do as an adult.

Murray was of average build with skin the color of freshly baked croissants and a kind face that reminded him of someone he couldn't quite place. Drew didn't know much about him, except that he ordered a blueberry muffin with coffee and walked like he was always on 'island time'.

Drew was always glad to see him. Murray usually came at a time when the commuter rush had thinned away and the bakery was quiet until the afternoon crowd came. Although Delites didn't encourage tips, Murray left one anyway. He spoke in a soft voice, but didn't give the appearance of a weak man, but a wise one.

"It's doing well," Drew said, trying to be humble, although he'd seen record growth.

"You're even smiling more now."

Drew knew that smile wasn't just because of the business. After getting a second opinion and eating more potassium rich foods and staying hydrated, his attacks had lessened. His new rheumatologist didn't have an exact cause yet, but did say Drew had inflammatory arthritic tendencies and would always have to be diligent in managing it. However, he didn't envision the crippling future Drew had imagined before.

Plus, he knew he had another reason to keep a smile on his face: Clarice. Having her in his life made him happier than he could put into words. He still remembered the sight of her face when he'd surprised her one evening with a red velvet cake.

She'd taken a bite then closed her eyes and moaned in pleasure. "You've ruined me for anyone else."

"That's the idea."

She took another bite, licking the icing from the corner of her mouth. "This is heavenly."

And watching her eat had taken him even higher. However he didn't want to tell Murray that and end up sounding like a love struck teenager. "Hmm."

"Heard you're famous now."

"Not really," Drew said, walking with Murray to an empty table. He'd gotten into the habit of talking to him for a few minutes before he went back to work. He'd also learned that taking a break after a tense morning helped his joints.

Murray took a sip of his coffee. "But you're traveling. I heard you did a big event in Chicago."

Drew wondered how he knew about that. Although he posted photos of the cakes he made online, he didn't think he'd put up the Chicago event yet. Maybe one of the clerks had told him. "Yes, it's fun."

"Running this business and traveling can't leave much room for a social life."

"I make room," he said, remembering the complaints he'd heard from Jennifer. He didn't hear the same ones from Clarice.

"Not many women would want to be second fiddle to a man's career."

"Mine understands."

Murray nodded impressed. "Support like that is golden."

"Hmm."

"But I'm sure you've got the talent to deliver as well."

"It's what I live for."

"Almost wish I had an event I could hire you for. I'm divorced and I don't celebrate birthdays anymore."

Drew laughed, surprised to realize he was even laughing more. "I know what you mean. The only events I celebrate are someone else's."

"And that's how you can lose what's important to you."

Drew's good mood dropped. "What?"

Murray took a bite of his muffin.

"What do you mean? You think I'll lose Clarice?"

"I didn't say that."

"You said I could lose something important."

"Perhaps I put it wrong. What I meant is don't confuse someone else's life with yours." When Drew frowned, Murray tried to explain further. "Has Clarice met your family yet?"

Drew felt his throat tighten and felt suddenly exposed. "No."

"Have you met hers?"

"No."

"Why not?"

"We've been busy."

"How long have you been seeing each other?"

Drew stood. He wouldn't have his conversation. His private life was none of this man's business no matter how much he liked him. He and Clarice had a solid relationship. "I'd better get back to work."

Murray took another bite, unfazed by Drew's cool tone. "I don't care if you're angry," he said. He lifted his gaze to Drew's. "As long as I gave you something to think about."

Chapter Twenty-one

Clarice stared at Drew as if he'd asked her to dance on top of a plane flying in mid-air. "You want me to meet your parents?" When he'd asked her to stop by the bakery after closing, having assured her that he wasn't in pain and just wanted to see her, she'd expected him to say something else. Now she stared at him across the table in the eatery section hardly able to believe her ears.

"Hmm."

"Why?"

He frowned. "Because that's what you do."

"Why has this thought come to you all of a sudden?"

He shrugged. "I just thought it was time."

"I haven't asked you to meet mine."

"Don't think I haven't noticed."

He'd hinted at wanting to meet her mother or father, but she'd always changed the subject. It would be complicated. Not even her sister knew she was seeing someone. "I'm just not sure it's a good idea yet."

"We've been seeing each other for nearly four months now, longer if you count before Jamaica."

Her face burned at the memory.

"And then there was Seattle." He winked.

"You don't have to remind me."

"And we took Theo to his favorite theme park. And we made pizza together last Friday."

Clarice nodded again. "I know that too."

"So there's no use pretending it's not serious between us."

"I wasn't trying to pretend that it wasn't."

"Theo really likes you."

She chewed her lip. "I know and I like him too." She folded her arms. "It's just a big step."

He nodded.

Clarice rested her palms flat on the table. "What did you tell them about me?"

"That you're someone I'm seeing."

"And?"

Drew shrugged. "And what?"

"Do they know how old I am? What I do for a living?"

"No."

"Why not?"

"Because they'll find out when they meet you." He reached out and tenderly touched her cheek. "Relax, it will be fine."

"It's going to be a disaster."

"Quiet Theo," Drew warned as he straightened his nephew's tie in his bedroom as they both prepared for the dinner at his parents' house.

"Granddad really liked Jennifer. What if they say something mean?"

"They won't."

"What if they scare her away? I don't want them to scare her away."

Drew stood then turned and checked his own reflection in the closet mirror. He wore dark trousers and a maroon sweater. Classic yet casual, just the way his parents liked it. "Clarice likes us. She won't get scared."

"Granddad can be scary. Does she *have* to meet them?"

Drew grabbed a jacket and put it on. "Yes."

Theo sat on the bed. "Why?"

"Because that's what you do. When you're dating, I'll meet whoever you're with."

"Not if I don't want you to," he muttered.

Drew turned to him. "What?"

"Nothing."

The doorbell rang.

Theo jumped off the bed. "That's her. You sure you won't change your mind?"

He walked to the door. They'd scheduled Clarice meet them at the apartment then he'd drive them to his parents' place since his place was in the same direction. "I'm sure."

In the car Theo remained anxious as the headlights of Drew's car pierced through the dark autumn evening, fallen leaves tumbling along the shoulder of the road. "And don't drop your tea cup into the saucer. You have to settle it down gently or Grandma gets upset. And keep your elbows off the table, and don't laugh too loud, and please don't mention Manchester United."

"What?" Clarice said.

Drew shook his head. "Ignore him."

Theo continued. "When it comes to football my Granddad can talk your ear off."

"He means soccer," Drew said.

Clarice smiled. "I figured as much. What else shouldn't I do?"

Drew shot her a glance. "Don't encourage him."

"Why not? I want to be prepared."

Theo tapped his chin. "That's all I can think of right now but if I think of anything else, I'll let you know."

"That's very kind of you. Since your uncle won't tell me anything."

"It's only 'cause nothing scares him."

"You think I should be scared?"

"No," Drew said.

"Very," Theo said.

Chapter Twenty-two

The moment Clarice met Mr. and Mrs. Cutter she understood why Theo had been frightened. Mr. Cutter looked as if he'd been carved out of onyx with dark eyes, a large build and broad shoulders. Although he wore business casual—light trousers and a blue shirt—they were ironed to perfection and didn't make him appear casual at all. His wife looked equally imposing with tiny pinched features crowded to the middle of her face and the look of a sadistic headmistress in an all black dress and dark green sweater.

Clarice flashed her brightest smile and greeted them warmly. They were cordial but didn't try to hide their assessing gaze. She couldn't tell whether she disappointed or pleased them, whether it was English politeness or disdain.

It was during the middle of the meal—chicken tikka masala served over a bed of white rice, mingling the scents of black pepper, ginger and paprika—that the questions began. "What do you do, Clarice?" Mrs. Cutter asked, speaking as though she were carrying marbles in her mouth.

"I'm sorry?"

"Your occupation, dear," Mrs. Cutter said speaking more slowly.

"I'm a CPA. I own a business with my mother."

"And she's helped Uncle a lot," Theo said.

His grandfather shot him a glance. "Are you speaking with your mouth full?"

Theo closed his mouth, shook his head and continued chewing.

"Is that how you met each other?" Mrs. Cutter asked. "Through your business? Heaven knows Andrew needs the help."

"Business is much better now," Drew said.

"So you've been trying to convince us for years," his mother said in a dismissive tone of pity. She turned to Clarice. "Did he tell you that he received a full scholarship to go to university? He had a brilliant mind and brilliant future ahead of him in computer science. And one summer he tells us he wants to quit to bake cookies."

Drew lifted his glass of wine. "That wasn't exactly how I put it."

"We keep waiting for him to come to his senses," Mr. Cutter said. "With diabetes on the rise, obesity and heart disease a major concern, he's not doing much to help the problem."

"I make people happy."

"So do pubs but they don't do anyone's liver any good, now do they?" his father said.

"Anything in moderation is fine," Clarice said, trying to be diplomatic. "I don't think indulging in a sweet treat is bad every once in a while. He's running a successful business that employs people and serves his community."

Mr. Cutter sniffed. "I see why you got rid of Jennifer for this one. She stands up for you like Stuart used to."

"I didn't get rid of Jennifer," Drew said in a dry tone. "It just didn't work out."

"Relationships take effort."

"I know that."

"She wanted the best for you and knows you have the potential to—"

"I don't care, which explains the reason why she's no longer with me."

Mrs. Cutter spoke up. "She came by the other day before I went to see Stuart."

Clarice, sensing the tension in the room, tried to change the subject. "Drew told me about him. I'm sorry for your loss."

Her face changed. "What loss?"

"Stuart's passing."

"Stuart isn't dead."

Clarice looked at Drew who avoided her gaze. "But I thought—"

"Never mind," his mother said with an impatient flick of the wrist. "It isn't your fault that my son has a macabre sense of humor."

Drew shook his head. "It's not a joke, Mum."

"Theo, you can go to the other room," Mr. Cutter said, making his request sound like a demand. Once the boy was out of the room he turned to his son and said, "You know better than that."

"I was just—"

"Let it go, Andrew."

The ominous tone of warning had no effect on his son. Drew looked at Clarice and said in a calm voice, "My brother had a grand mal seizure."

"And he's in the hospital recovering," his father clarified.

"He's not going to recover."

"You can be a pessimist but we won't."

"He's been in a coma for more than a year. No brain activity."

"He's had seizures all his life," Mrs. Cutter said to Clarice, poignantly ignoring her son. "This last one was quite bad."

"We tried everything from medication to surgery," his father continued, "but nothing worked. This last seizure was the one—"

"That killed him," Drew said.

His father stood. "Your brother isn't dead."

Drew surged to his feet and met his glare. "He might as well be."

His father slapped him hard. Enough to draw blood. He instantly regretted it. "Andrew—"

Drew tenderly touched his lip. "If you wanted me to leave, you could have just asked."

His father reached for him. "I didn't mean—"

"It's all right, Dad." He turned to leave.

"Please don't go," his mother said.

"I think I should. I wouldn't want to bleed all over your good china." He left the room.

Clarice followed him into the hallway. "Please don't leave like this. I'm sorry I said anything."

Drew made his way to the powder room. "It's not your fault." He turned on the faucet. "I forgot to warn you."

Clarice reached for a hand towel to dab at his cut, he lightly slapped her hand away. "Put that back. I don't need you to nurse me and that's Mum's favorite set."

She returned the towel then wiped away a tear before it fell down her cheek. "We're both in the same boat in a strange way."

Drew turned off the faucet then dried his hands. "How?"

"Your parents want you to act as if your brother's alive and my mother wants me to act as if my sister's dead."

"Why?"

Clarice stared at him. He didn't know? He didn't re-member? Since the event loomed so large in her mind, since it was so unforgettable, she never considered that he may not know all the details as to why the wedding had been cancelled. Or if he had known then, that he could forget it.

"I'll tell you later. It's a long story. Let's just say we have a lot in common."

"Yes, family is a funny thing."

"But I like your parents."

His brows shot up. "Those dull, stuffy people in the dining room?"

"Yes."

He grinned. "You mean they didn't scare you?"

"No."

"What's there to like?"

"I'm being serious, Drew. I like them and if we leave now, they may not feel the same way about me."

"Right now I don't care." He left the powder room.

"I'd hate to cause a rift."

"The rift is already there." He lightly touched her cheek, seeing her worried expression. "Don't worry we usually come around."

"Please. I don't want a nice evening to end on such an awful note."

Drew thought for a moment then sighed and narrowed his eyes. "It means that much to you?"

"Yes."

He pointed at her. "I'm only doing this for you."

"Thank you." She turned.

He grabbed her wrist and pulled her back. "I'm sacrific-ing myself for you. I want more than your thanks."

"I'm not kissing a man with a busted lip."

"It's not that busted."

Clarice wrapped her arms around his neck and whispered in his ear. "I'll make your sacrifice worth it later."

Chapter Twenty-three

An awkward silence greeted their return to the table, but Clarice managed to bring up a neutral topic that for a while eased the tension. Theo returned to the table and they finished dinner then had dessert, before another dangerous topic entered the conversation.

"How's Theo doing in school?" Mr. Cutter asked after Theo had been excused to play a game in another room.

"Well," Drew said.

"You know our offer is still open."

Drew shook his head and sighed. "Not now Dad."

"You're a young man, trying to run your business. I think Theo would have a more stable environment staying here with us."

"Thanks for the offer, but Stuart left me as guardian. He made that clear. And Theo's doing well with me right now."

"For how long?"

"You tell me," Drew said in a low voice. "When do you expect Stuart to wake up?"

His father glared at him then looked at Clarice. "This is no offense to you. You seem like a charming woman. But so were the other two he's already introduced to us." He returned his gaze to his son. "How many women will you expose him to?"

"There haven't been that many. I've been too busy—"

"Exactly. You're always busy and a boy like Theo needs care not a housekeeper parading as a nanny. You still owe us—"

"I know you've paid Gladys for the past three months and I'll pay you back. Gladys works well with my schedule and Theo likes her."

"You wouldn't need her if—"

"Theo stays with me."

"We could fight you on this."

Drew looked as if his father had struck him again, except with a deeper blow. Clarice had never seen such a look of betrayal and pain on his face before. "Yes," he said in a whisper. "You could."

Clarice hated the fear she saw and knew she had to act. "We were going to tell you later, we're engaged."

The Cutters blinked in surprised, his father spoke first. "I'm sorry?"

"It's something that we've been discussing. I have a townhouse and a stable job so that Theo could stay at the same school and when Drew travels he wouldn't have to worry. I'd wanted to have a family and at my age why wait?"

His parents stared at her then slowly turned to him. "Is this true?" Mrs. Cutter asked.

He hesitated.

"Drew's upset with me because we haven't ironed all the details out yet," Clarice said with a nervous laugh. "But I can assure you that Theo's care has always been at the forefront of his mind. He told me—"

"Stop," Drew said, shaking his head. "I saw you do this with Jennifer, but not here. Don't paint a picture of me that isn't real."

"Just let me—"

"I'm not going to pretend." He faced his parents. "No, we're not engaged. If you want to fight me for custody, that is your decision. But just once I'd like you to trust me. No," he said, his voice shaking with emotion. "I demand that you let me honor my brother's wishes. Don't take that away from me because that's all I have left." He swallowed. "Please."

"Andrew—," his father began but his mother cut him off and said, "Okay."

Clarice stood. "I'll go get Theo and tell him we're ready to leave. Thank you for a wonderful meal."

"Doubt the pudding lived up to what Andrew makes," Mrs. Cutter said.

"It was delicious," Clarice said, now seeing that the other woman's tight features hid a sad heart.

She went into the other room surprised not to see Theo playing with the game console his grandparents had bought specifically for him when he came to visit, but instead staring at the ground, pacing.

"What is it?" she asked.

He stopped pacing and looked up at her. "I'm not loyal. Uncle taught me it's important to be loyal."

She knelt in front of him. "Who says you're not loyal?"

"I know I'm not."

"Why?"

His eyes filled with tears. "Because." He wiped his eyes.

She softened her voice. "Because…why?"

"Sometimes I think Granddad is right and my dad will wake up. But if I'm wrong then Uncle will be mad at me that I didn't believe him and then he won't trust me and then he won't like me and then he won't want me to live with him anymore and I do like living with him but some-times…sometimes…"

"You miss your dad."

He nodded.

"I think your uncle would understand that."

Tears streamed down his cheeks. "But he doesn't think Dad will wake up."

"No, but hoping for something you want doesn't make you disloyal. Your uncle loves you very much and I know he'd never want you to be unhappy. It's okay to miss your dad, to wish you could be with him. That doesn't mean you love your uncle less." She opened her arms. "Come here."

He fell into her arms and cried. "I wish everything could be like it was," he said into her chest. "I wish we could all be happy again."

Clarice stroked his back, thinking how often she'd wished that for her own family. How many times she'd wished the wedding day had never happened. How she wished she had the power to turn back time. "I know."

Chapter Twenty-four

"Like chalk and cheese you two," May Cutter said to her husband as they washed and dried the dishes. "You couldn't let pudding pass without riling him up. Why did you have to bring up the boy?"

"It was on my mind," Jon Cutter said without apology, drying a plate. "Don't tell me you aren't worried too."

"It was best left for another day."

Jon took a glass and dried it, a wistful look entering his features. "That boy is looking more like Stuart every day. Smart like him too."

"But he's not."

Jon sighed, setting the glass down. "I know. I was just making a statement."

"What do you think of her?"

"She seems to have her head on her shoulders."

May carefully rinsed soap off of a dish. "What do you think she sees in him? She's older and she certainly makes more."

"You don't know that."

She handed her husband the dish. "I noticed the clothes. Don't be fooled by the simplicity of her look. That tailored skirt didn't come cheap; neither did her earrings or shoes."

Jon shrugged. "I doubt she sees him as a toy boy."

"And don't you wonder what he sees in her?"

"No. I liked her."

May unplugged the sink and dried her hands. "You always like them."

"It's easier that way. Fortunately, he's right. There haven't been that many."

"True."

They left the kitchen and sat in the living room where pictures of their immediate and extended family hung on the walls and gathered on the mantle over the fireplace.

"She's different than the others," Jon said, resting his arm along the back of the couch.

May leaned against him. "I noticed that too."

"Do you think it may be serious?"

"On his side yes," May said, sending her husband a worried look. "But I'm not sure about her."

"She tried to get us to believe that they were engaged."

"I know, that's what worries me. A woman who can lie so easily isn't someone you can trust."

"She was doing it for his sake."

"Or does she have another agenda?"

"Our Andrew doesn't have a lot to offer yet."

"That's what worries me. I think a woman like her may break his heart."

Chapter Twenty-five

She was hiding.

Clarice hadn't seen Drew since the dinner with his parents two weeks ago. She told herself it was because she'd gotten busy, that their schedules didn't match. She didn't want to admit that it had hurt her that he hadn't even wanted to pretend that they were going to get married. That he'd embarrassed her by not playing along.

She wondered if she felt more for him than he did for her and then felt foolish for her feelings. The rosy picture she'd given had sounded good to her. Too good. Perhaps it wasn't something he even saw in the future. At least not with her.

She wanted to give herself space so that she could analyze her feelings. It had been a while since she'd felt this happy with someone, maybe she was putting too much pressure on him. Perhaps space was something they both needed. And she had grown attached to Theo. Would it be fair to him if she was suddenly out of his life?

When Drew sent a text, demanding to see her (a request he rarely made without reason), Clarice wasn't surprised. She kept her voice light when she called him and scheduled a time and place. Maybe he sensed a change too. If he wanted to end things she understood. She'd miss him, but it was the sensible path. She'd had her fun. Glorious, wonderful fun but she'd never expected it to last.

When he arrived she welcomed him to her backyard to sit under a sugar maple whose leaves still clung to branches in an array of yellow and orange hues. The unseasonably warm day also welcomed the sight of a robin hopping along the ground.

"I thought the weather was nice," Clarice said motioning to the bench, answering a question he hadn't asked. She didn't want to separate inside her house, the memory would linger there.

He sat down then stared up at her. "Was Theo right?"

"What?"

"Did my parents scare you away?"

Clarice slowly sank down beside him. "No."

"Then why do I get the feeling you've been avoiding me?"

"I've been busy."

Drew took a deep breath. "I know what you were trying to do that night with them. I know you were trying to help me," he said coming straight to the point, "but I don't ever want you to do something like that again. Marriage is not something I joke about."

Clarice nodded, feeling the weight of his words. If this was why he wanted to break up with her that was fine. She wouldn't fight him. "I understand. I'm sorry."

"And I wouldn't marry a woman just because she's

financially stable, has a house and lives in a kid friendly district."

She nodded again, fighting back tears, not wanting to admit how much his words hurt. "Drew, I know I made a mistake."

He tenderly cupped her face. "The woman I decide to marry will know how much I want her. How precious she is to me and she'll know that I don't care what she has. And when I ask her to marry me, everyone will know because I like to live my life truthfully." He bit his lip, searching her eyes. "And whoever I decide to marry, I want them to feel the same."

Clarice nodded unable to speak, unable to make any promises. "Have you talked to them since then?"

"Yes," he said, but that one word held a load of meaning. He looked as if he'd gone through a battle, looked defeated, tired and sad. "The good news is that they liked you."

"You've got bags under your eyes."

He hung his head for a moment as if gathering his courage then turned to her and said, "Because I missed you."

She hugged him, wanting to comfort him; sorry that she hadn't let him explain before. *I missed you too.* "I just needed time to think."

He held her close. "Just tell me what you think next time."

"I will."

"Clarice?" someone called from the front of the house. Clarice stiffened as she heard the sound of heels clicking along the brick path. Soon she'd hear the swing of the back gate. Someone was coming.

Drew tightened his arms around her and whispered, "Don't let go."

But she wanted to. She wanted to run. To hide. To not face who was coming or even what was coming. The looks, the questions. Why was he asking her to stay? He didn't know what was at risk. What she could lose.

"Please," he said softly, sensing her hesitation.

And in her fear she felt his need. Felt her own need too. He wanted her, but she wanted him just as much. She didn't want to hide in the shadows forever. Her mother or sister would have to know about him one day. *But. But. But,* her mind screamed and though she wanted to run she didn't move.

"Oh," a surprised voice said and Clarice felt her tension ease knowing it was the voice of her sister. Not the one she truly feared.

She drew away from Drew and faced Faiza, seeing the curiosity bright in her gaze. "This is Drew."

Her sister gave him an appreciative once over and flashed Clarice a 'go sister' smile. She held out her hand. "Faiza, nice to meet you."

"Same," Drew said.

"So how long has this been going on?"

"A few months," Clarice said.

"Does Mom know?"

"Not yet."

"Don't look at me like that," Faiza said with a laugh. "Considering we're not speaking, your secret is safe with me. Although I don't know why you'd want to keep this one."

"Did you need me for something?" Clarice said, uncomfortable with her sister eying Drew as if he were the last key lime pie at a bake sale.

"Just came by to say hi. Carl's with the kids today and I thought we could do something."

Drew turned to Clarice. "And Theo's at a friend's so I'm free as well." He clasped his hands together. "I'd love the chance to treat you two ladies to lunch."

"That's not necessary," Clarice said.

"That's wonderful," Faiza countered.

He looked at them both. "What's the verdict?"

Faiza looped her arm through his. "I'm starving and know the perfect place."

Chapter Twenty-six

She monopolized him. It was something that Faiza did best and Clarice didn't mind the attention her sister demanded from Drew. It gave her a chance to think things through. Would meeting her sister be enough for him? If so, then he wouldn't need to meet her mother any time soon. He and Faiza were very similar—they ordered the same appetizer (loaded potato skins) and lunch (black bean burger)—and seemed to get on well. That may prove a problem. Her mother may not like how forthright he could be.

Too bad a wicked little voice said. But her more rational side knew it best to keep them apart a little while longer.

"So how did you two meet?" Faiza asked.

Before Clarice could stop him, Drew said, "At a wedding."

"Really? Whose?"

"Mom's," Clarice said.

Faiza swore. "You're kidding me."

"He was the caterer."

Drew shook his head. "I was with the company. I was an apprentice at the time."

Faiza frowned. "Wait, how old are you?"

"Twenty-seven."

She stared at Clarice. "He's seven years *younger*? Mom is going to have a fit."

"I'll be twenty-eight in November."

Faiza shook her head. "Trust me that won't make a difference."

"We're taking things slow," Clarice said. "He doesn't need to be introduced to her yet."

"You better not tell her how you met then."

"I won't. Besides, it wasn't really at the wedding. It was after and it's a long story."

"Actually we did," Drew said.

"We did what?"

"Meet at the wedding. You kissed me."

Clarice stared at him stunned. "No, I didn't."

"Yes, you did."

Clarice looked at her sister and laughed. "He's making things up."

"You were on your cell phone then hung up and saw me. I came to ask you something about the reception and you said 'I'm so happy I have to kiss someone' and you did. Me."

She'd totally forgotten that. Yes, she remembered the reception was to be right next door and she was with the flurry of people getting it ready. The memory of the wedding had erased anything before it and now she slowly remembered. That was when she had gotten the phone call she'd had with Luisa and the chance she'd been given. She'd practiced what she was going to say to her mother. She would finally be free to live her life. She'd planned to tell her mother before she left to go on her honeymoon. But after the phone call she'd been bursting with energy and remembered seeing a young man walking with a tray. He was wearing a cap over his head so she couldn't see his eyes. And she'd been uncharacteristically rash.

Faiza's brows shot up. "My sister kissed you?"

He nodded.

"Where?"

He tapped the side of his face. "On the cheek."

Faiza laughed. "That sounds like her. Even impulsively she's demure. I would have kissed you right on the mouth." She turned to her sister. "Why did you kiss him anyway?"

"I don't remember," Clarice lied. "The day didn't end well."

Faiza shrugged. "I didn't plan it."

Drew leaned forward and looked at the two women. "Is there something I should know?"

"Not really," Clarice said.

"I married my mother's fiancé," Faiza said.

Drew's face split into a wide smile. He looked at Clarice and jerked his head at Faiza. "Is that another way to tell me to mind my own business?"

"No," Clarice said. "She's telling you the truth."

His smile fell. "Wait I heard the wedding was canceled because of some mix-up."

"You could say that. My sister told the groom she loved him and he left with her."

Drew looked at Faiza amazed. "You ran off with your mother's fiancé on her wedding day?"

"I know my timing was off," she said with some defiance, "but my mother and Carl would have made a terrible mistake. He tried to tell her that, but she refused to hear it. We're still together and very happy,"

Drew cleared his throat. "I see."

Faiza sipped her drink. "So now you understand why you'd better come up with a better way to explain how you two met."

"If he meets her at all," Clarice said.

"Why wouldn't I meet her?" Drew asked.

Why indeed, she almost wished she'd kept her mouth shut. Faiza had no such problem.

"Because she's miserable and wants everyone around her to be miserable too."

"That's not why."

"Then why haven't you been with anyone since—"

"I think it's time to go."

"I haven't finished eating."

Clarice prepared to leave. "Then I'll let you two enjoy yourselves."

Drew covered her hand. "Clarice, wait."

"Let her go," Faiza said. "The wedding is always a sore spot."

Clarice glared at her. "It's more than a sore spot."

"Only because you let Mom make you feel guilty for something you didn't do."

"Maybe because someone should feel guilty."

"I've forgiven myself. It's the only way to go on. They would have been miserable together."

"You could have run off with him sooner. You didn't have to hurt her on her wedding day."

"Sometimes you go on as if she's a saint. Like she's never hurt anyone. How do you think Dad felt when she divorced him out of the blue?"

Clarice paused. "So you chose her wedding day as some sort of revenge for Dad?"

"I didn't say that. I told you it was spur of the moment. But—"

Clarice pushed her chair back. "I'm not having this conversation."

Faiza blinked, devastated. "After all these years, you still haven't forgiven me?"

Clarice felt instantly contrite. "It's not that simple. I know why you did it. And I know how Carl felt pressured, I just wish—" She saw Drew looking at them with interest and shook her head. "Never mind."

Faiza sighed, resigned. "You don't have to leave. I will. Just pack this up for me and drop it off later." She looked at Drew. "It was fascinating meeting you."

He nodded. "Likewise."

She kissed him on the cheek, stood then motioned for her sister to follow. "Stop being a coward," she said when Drew was out of hearing.

"What?"

"I know we don't have a lot in common, but this is the best advice I can give you."

"I'm not a coward."

"Yes, you are. You've never risked anything for love. Not for a passion or for another person. You hide and blame. But I refuse to live like that."

Tears stung Clarice's eyes. "Never risked anything? Do you think throwing away a chance at a dream career isn't a risk?"

"What dream career?"

"Never mind. It doesn't matter now because I loved Mom so much that I gave it up for her."

"Sacrifice isn't risk. It's surrender. Surrender to a life filled with regrets. You should be with Drew no matter what Mom or anyone else says. Throwing him away won't change anything with her. It won't make her happier. It will just make you more miserable." She glanced over at Drew. "But the choice is up to you." She sauntered away.

Clarice composed herself before she returned to the table.

Drew read her expression. "I guess lunch was a bad idea."

Yes. Terrible. "No, it wasn't your fault."

"Why don't you want me to meet your mother?"

"Isn't one family member enough?"

"I'm just curious."

"Don't be."

"I can't help it," he said his voice deepening. "I'm curious about everything about you."

She couldn't stop a smile. "A little mystery is a good thing."

"I like solving mysteries."

"You'll have to wait to solve this one," she said then kissed two fingers and pressed them against his lips.

"Aww, isn't that cute," Faiza said, lifting the purse she'd left on the back of her chair. "You look like you're kissing your nephew."

It was a low blow and hit its target. Clarice felt her face grow hot then cold with embarrassment, tears touching her eyes. She knew she wasn't as openly affectionate as her sister; that her tenderness seemed quaint to others, but her feelings for Drew were real and deep and it hurt to have them taunted and scrutinized. In one sentence her sister had mocked their age difference and affection.

"Sit down," Drew said in a low voice. "Now," he added when Faiza began to open her mouth to protest.

She sat.

"That was uncalled for."

"That came out wrong," Faiza admitted. "I was just—"

"Embarrassing your mother wasn't enough so you need to embarrass your sister too?"

Faiza rested a hand on her chest, stunned. "I wasn't trying to embarrass anyone. Honest. I really think you two look cute together."

"It's okay," Clarice said in a low voice, quickly blinking back tears. "She didn't mean any harm."

"Didn't she?" he said in a sharp tone.

Clarice met his gaze, silently pleading with him to let it pass. She didn't want them fighting. "No."

Drew nodded, his jaw twitching. "Okay." He looked at Faiza. "You'd better go before I decide to leave you with the bill."

"I really didn't mean—"

He waved at her. "Bye."

She sighed then left.

Clarice closed her eyes. "Don't be angry with her. She can be thoughtless sometimes, but it's not malicious."

"Then why did she make you cry?"

"She didn't. She always gets a little snappy when we talk about the wedding and it makes me sad."

"Why do you keep defending her?"

Clarice released a hollow laugh, but was unable to give him an answer.

Chapter Twenty-seven

It took her two hours, a black coffee and biscotti to finally gather up the courage to confront her sister. Rarely did Clarice allow herself to get angry at Faiza, but the comment she'd made at lunch with Drew made her blood boil every time she thought of it. She could make fun of Clarice, but dragging Drew into her teasing was crossing the line. In the past she would have waited weeks before she shared how she felt, but this time Clarice didn't want to wait.

She knocked on the front door of Faiza's and Carl's blue colonial, holding the remnants of Faiza's lunch Clarice had agreed to drop off.

She silently practiced what she would say and when the door swung open she started to begin, but her words died on her lips when she saw her sister's panicked expression. Then her gaze fell to the limp baby boy she held cradled in her hands. "Thank God you're here," Faiza said. "He's barely breathing and I don't know what to do. He's done this before, but usually he comes around."

"Where's Carl?" Clarice asked, stepping into the house.

"He left to run an errand. I'm so scared."

"Have you called the ambulance?"

"No, I—"

Clarice pulled out her cell phone and started to dial. She listened to the operator's instructions while they waited for the EMTs who arrived within minutes and whisked mother and son away while Clarice stayed behind to look after Maggie and Tulip.

After a brief phone call with Carl who'd joined his wife at the hospital, Clarice learned that little Stone's heart had been in distress, but they'd managed to get it working again. However, he would need more tests to find out what was going on.

Hours later, Faiza returned from the hospital with her husband and a sleeping Stone.

"He's been sickly," Faiza told Clarice as they sat in the living room once the children were all in bed. "He's never been as strong as his sister. The doctors don't know what's wrong. What if…"

Clarice patted her back. "We'll find out what's wrong."

Faiza covered her face. "This is when I wish I could talk to Mom."

Clarice stiffened. "I don't think that would change any-thing."

Faiza let her hands fall and turned to her. "Could you talk to her? Tell her about Stone?"

Clarice shook her head. "Faiza. I can't."

"Why not?"

"Because…because I want to introduce Drew to her and that will be stressful enough. I can't add this on top of it."

"Do you really believe that introducing her to your *boyfriend* is more important than this?"

Clarice didn't like the way her sister stressed the word boyfriend, as if Drew were some toy she wanted to show off. "That's not what I said. But Drew and Theo mean a lot to me and I—"

"Stone could die. Do you realize that? He could die and I'd hate for him to leave us without Mom ever knowing about him. I don't mean to put you in the middle of this, but this is about family. Family should pull together in times of crisis." She grabbed her hand, her tone beseeching. "Please, I wouldn't ask you to do this if I didn't think it wasn't important."

"Faiza—"

"Maybe this is my punishment. Our punishment, Carl and me, for being so happy. We never meant to hurt anyone truly. I don't want to live this way anymore. This is a chance to change it. To be together again. Just tell her, please."

Clarice briefly closed her eyes torn between her sister's need and her desire to protect her mother. "I can't promise anything, but—"

Faiza hugged her. "Thank you. I knew you'd understand."

Minutes later Clarice sat in her car and pounded her fists on the steering wheel rage and resentment warring inside her. It wasn't fair. She'd again been robbed of her glory. She'd wanted to tell Faiza how she truly felt then Stone got sick; she wanted to share her joy about Drew, but Faiza needed her mother. Why did she always seem to be on the losing end?

Clarice rested her head on the steering wheel, fighting against tears. Her sister had given her a nearly impossible task. She wanted to have Clarice ask her mother to care about something—someone—when she hadn't cared about anything in years. She felt beaten and worn and longed for only one thing.

Chapter Twenty-eight

Drew didn't usually slam doors. But when he arrived at his apartment and got out of his car, he slammed the door with extra force. He'd screwed up again. He'd thought by meeting Clarice's sister, he could protect their relationship from Murray's warning. He thought by charming her perhaps Clarice would want to introduce him to her parents as well; instead he'd made her cry. Not directly. He had her sister to blame for that, but indirectly.

He'd even put his foot in it by mentioning the wedding. Why hadn't he just mentioned the birthday party instead of something that had happened eight years ago? Just because it had seared itself in his mind hadn't made it special. But it was a day that had changed things for him.

This beautiful, amazing woman had kissed him and made him laugh and he'd lied to her—again! It hadn't been on the cheek. It had been a full-on kiss. On his mouth. Her lips touching his—brief, spicy, delicious—in a way he'd always remember. And he remembered spinning away and wanting to follow her.

But that day hadn't ended well for her. And she barely remembered him when he later arrived at her office with the invoice, not that he could blame her. And it was even more ridiculous that he thought she'd remember him—or rather that kiss—all these years later. He felt like such a fool. It was a moment he should have kept to himself.

He remembered the look of shock that Faiza had when she spoke about their age difference. Why did it matter? It wasn't that much. Why would it bother their mother? He was employed, he cared about her. Wasn't that enough?

Drew walked into the apartment and patted Lady who greeted him at the door, surprised by how quiet the place was until he remembered Theo had asked if he could sleepover at his friend's house. He was glad. He didn't want his nephew seeing him like this. He was usually so smooth, but Clarice always seemed to throw him off balance. He always seemed to be making the wrong move. Say the wrong thing. And if he kept making the wrong choices he'd ruin what they had.

He sat down on the couch and turned on the TV then selected a movie to watch just for the noise.

He scowled when he heard a knock on the door when he'd started his second film—one he'd seen before and didn't like, but was too lazy to search for something else— and stood up. He swung open the door then froze when he saw Clarice.

She peeked behind him. "Is Theo here? Because I just—"

Drew kissed away the rest of her sentence, closing the door behind her. He didn't care why she came, didn't want to talk, didn't want to do anything but touch her, taste her, hold her in his arms. He wanted to remove her sister's catty words from his memory 'aww so cute. You look like you're kissing your nephew.'

He'd never kissed any aunty like this. Never kissed any woman like this with his whole heart bare for anyone to see. He let his mouth trail down her neck.

"Drew, wait," Clarice said when he swept her up in his arms, coat, handbag and all and walked to the bedroom, turning on the lights.

"Don't worry." He set her down and removed her jacket. "Theo's not here," he said, quickly undressing her then himself, not wanting anything to separate them. Not fabric or time or age or family. He wanted her close, to feel her skin pressed against his. He wanted to make sure she knew she was his.

As they fell onto the mattress, he felt the power of his domain. Here he was master. Alone with her he wouldn't make a mistake and he could be free to let her know how he felt.

Clarice rested a hand on his chest. "Drew, wait. Stop."

His heart began to race, this was too important to him. He didn't want her pushing him away. "Why?"

"You have nothing to prove."

She made his face burn, revealing his insecurity, but he wouldn't admit it. It was more than that. He wasn't just thinking of Faiza, but of anyone who would try to pull them apart. He was man enough for her. She was perfect for him. That was the only declaration he wanted to make. He kissed her again this time with more heated passion. He was no longer angry, but hungry. Hungry for her.

"Please don't tell me to stop," he said. "I want you to touch me all over."

"I think I've already done that."

"Find new places."

"But—"

"Please, Clarice. I want this. I want you." He pressed his lips against the inside of her throat. "Don't push me away."

"I'm not. I just want you to slow down. There's no need to rush. I'm not going anywhere. Take your time."

"I don't think I can."

"Then let me show you how." She let her hand slide a slow, sensuous path down his chest. "Like this. Can you try that?"

"No, show me again."

Her hand gradually made its way down his thigh. "Like you're a driver wanting to enjoy the view."

He grinned, placing his hand on the curve of her hip then her stomach before slowly inching it up. "So, you're like a road and right now I'm going fifteen in a forty-five?"

"Yes, that's it."

He covered one breast then the other. "And I go even slower over the bumps."

"Exactly."

He slid his hand down to her pelvis. "And I have to stop at the fork in the road."

"Do you have any idea which way you want to go?" Clarice asked with a smile.

"Not yet, I'm just looking."

"Not much to see. You only have two options. Right or left."

"No, I see a third one."

"Really?"

He nodded. "Straight through." He snaked his hand down and cupped her center.

"That's a pretty short trip," Clarice said with a little gasp of surprise and thrilling pleasure that shot through her body when he made use of his fingers. She moved away from him so that she could focus. "I need to teach you some patience." She lightly skimmed her hand over the contours of his chest. "To enjoy the view and take in the sights a little longer." She touched his nipple and felt him stiffen. "What?"

"I get nervous when you touch me there."

Clarice laughed. "Don't be," she said lazily drawing little circles around one before she kissed it. "All better now?"

"It wasn't that one."

She kissed the other one. "This one?"

"Hmm."

"Hold on a moment." She got her handbag and pulled out a condom.

His mouth curved into a smile. "You came prepared. But I have—"

She pressed a finger against his lips. "I wasn't sure you'd have enough. I like long drives." She slid the condom on him. "Especially the feel of the gearshift," she said, rubbing her hand up and down the length of him.

Drew groaned deep in his throat. "You won't be driving slow if you keep touching it like that."

Clarice rubbed her thumb against his tip. "Don't worry, I know how to handle this machine." She settled herself on top of him. "I know how to make it hum," she said, tightening around him, letting him fill her inside. He was all she wanted right now. All she needed. He was all she thought about as she left her sister's house. With him she didn't have to lie or tap down her feelings, there was no holding back. With him she felt in control, powerful. She shifted her hips allowing him deeper inside, her body hot with liquid fire. "I know how to speed it up and how to slow it down."

"This machine might surprise you."

"Surprises can be for later."

His heated gaze met hers, not in challenge, but in surrender. "What do you want it to do right now?" he said in a deep voice.

"Take me on a ride as if we had all the time in the world."

Clarice lay under the sheets, her head on Drew's shoulder, her body limp with pleasure. "I can't believe it was you."

Drew didn't misunderstand her. "You remember it now?"

"Yes. I'd been so happy that day. Until…" A tear slid down her face and dripped on his chest. She quickly wiped it away, annoyed that those feelings were still so close to the surface. "I'm sorry."

He tenderly covered her hand with his. "Don't be. What was the phone call about?"

"My mentor was offering me a job. Something I'd dreamed about. But after what happened to Mom, I knew I couldn't take it."

"Why not?"

"I couldn't abandon her. She needed me."

"And she still needs you now?"

Clarice pressed her lips against his, quickly darting her tongue in his mouth. "That's how I should have kissed you that day."

He frowned, but his arm drew her closer. "You're changing the subject again."

"And like this." She licked his lower lip.

"That would have gotten you in trouble."

"I remember that you smelled like white chocolate and strawberries."

Drew couldn't help a smile. "You remember that?"

"The day seemed bright, wonderful, and beautiful and everyone in it. And now I have you here. I'm happy with you. That's why I wanted to see you."

"I'm glad you did."

He'd once thought he could only feel this content, this alive in the kitchen, surrounded by the smell of flour and sugar, the heat of an oven, the sound of a mixer, but for the first time he felt at home in his own skin with another person. He'd been at odds with his family; the women in his life were fun, but fleeting; his employees saw him as a hot shot baker who had a way with the ladies but with Clarice he felt like himself. She'd known about his mysterious attacks, how he'd misjudged Gerry, the affect of the loss of his brother and instead of feeling threatened, like his world could crumble at any moment, he felt as if a weight had been lifted.

But something about her smile seemed sad. "What is it?"

"I wanted to confront Faiza about what happened at lunch but…"

Clarice lowered her gaze and sighed in a way that made him want to keep out the world and protect her. She'd lifted a weight from his shoulders and he wanted to do the same. "Go on," he urged when she stopped.

"But her little boy is really sick. She ended up taking him to the hospital today."

"Will he be okay?"

"He's back at home now, but I don't know how thing will go in the long run."

He held her close. "I'm sorry. That must have been scary."

"It was but…" Clarice gripped her hand into a fist. "I'm angry too," she said surprised she'd been able to admit it aloud. Something she'd never allowed herself to say in the past. "I'm so angry." *I'm angry that it happened at all because I…I wanted to introduce you to my mother and now I can't. Because Stone's sick and Faiza wants me to tell Mom and I don't know how she's going to react.*

"How bad is he?"

"We don't know what's wrong with him yet."

"What do you want me to do?"

I don't know! I feel like I'm being ripped apart. I can't be in the middle of this forever. But I'm scared that I may lose you. That you won't understand. But I'm afraid I'll lose them too. "Just hold me."

"That's easy," Drew said, gathering her close. "What else?"

She closed her eyes, wondering if he'd be the one person in her life who didn't need something from her. She rested in the comfort of his embrace knowing she'd need strength to face what was ahead. *Love me no matter what.* "Nothing," she said with a sigh. "This is enough."

Chapter Twenty-nine

Her mother didn't take the news well, although that didn't surprise her. Clarice had decided to talk to her mother after treating her to a movie and light dinner. They now sat in the sparsely filled restaurant while a light drizzle of rain tapped against the windows.

Lois set down her fork, against her plate of spicy shrimp and noodles. "What did you just say?"

"Faiza wants to see you. Her baby is sick and—"

Lois held up her hand. "She's afraid he might die?"

Clarice nodded, her lips still tingling from the spicy dish they shared.

A cruel smile touched her lips. "Then she'll know what loss feels like."

"Mom, I'm serious."

"So am I. I have nothing to give her. Nothing more I should say. I gave her life, she took my man and I died eight years ago. There's nothing more. Why would you tell me this?"

"I just thought—"

"About her. It's always been about her."

"Don't be mean," Clarice said with a tired shake of her head. "I've been by your side all these years."

"Don't think I don't know that you visit her. That you don't care about her betrayal."

"Just because I see her doesn't mean I don't care. I love you both. I can't choose sides."

Lois rested her napkin on the table as if throwing down a gauntlet. "I want you to start now."

"I'm seeing someone," Clarice said, changing the topic, hoping to take her mother off-guard and not force her to make a choice.

Lois blinked. "What?"

"His name is Drew Cutter and I want to invite you over for dinner to meet him."

"And why should I meet him?"

"Because your opinion matters."

"But not enough."

"Please Mom."

Lois studied her for a moment. "Why are you only telling me about him now?"

"It wasn't serious before now."

"What does he do?"

"He's a wedding cake designer."

"What does that mean?"

"He's a baker."

Her brows shot up. "Is that why you took up baking?"

"Hmm," Clarice said quickly remembering her lie about taking lessons. "And he's younger than I am but not by much."

"How much?"

"Seven years."

"He's twenty-seven?"

"He'll be twenty-eight in November."

"And you'll be thirty-five in—"

"I know Mom."

Lois nodded. "That was clever."

Clarice paused surprised by her mother's change in tone. "What?"

"To shock me with the news of your sister so that I would be easier to persuade about your new man."

Clarice shook her head. "That's not why—"

"It doesn't matter. I look forward to meeting him. I expect he'll bake something delicious."

A lemon cake sat half eaten on Drew's dining room table.

"That was wonderful," Lois said, resting her fork down and cleaning the corners of her mouth with a napkin.

Drew grinned. "Thank you."

"My uncle can bake anything," Theo said. "You should come by the shop."

Lois nodded. "I'll remember that."

Theo threw his arms out wide. "People all around the world want his cakes."

"Not exactly," Drew said embarrassed by his nephew's enthusiasm. "But thanks to Clarice's help my name has spread. I was really struggling before her. I think for the first time in years I'll be solidly in the black instead of inching there."

"Do you have plans to grow?" Lois asked.

"No. Right now my focus is the business and keeping this kid out of trouble," he said affectionately nudging Theo with his elbow.

"Doesn't leave a lot of room for romance."

"I always leave room for things that are important to me."

"But sometimes even they get short shifted," Lois said, offering a soft challenge.

Drew didn't back down, keeping his tone equally soft. "Not in my life."

Clarice lifted up the cake knife. "Would anyone like seconds?"

At the end of the evening, while Theo and Drew cleared up, Clarice walked her mother to her car, eager to hear her verdict.

"He's a very charming young man," Lois said.

Clarice felt the knot in her chest ease. "I'm glad you liked him."

"I do. Very much." She stopped walking and touched her daughter's cheek. "And that's why I feel sorry for you."

Clarice took a step back as if her mother had slapped her. "What?"

Lois shook her head in pity. "You're as blind as I was back then."

"It's not the same. The age difference—"

Lois folded her arms and tilted her head. "I'm not talking about the age difference. It's not even as close to the seventeen years that separated Carl and me. No, I remember when I first met him. He was just starting his freelance career as a photographer. I was one of his first clients and he seemed so lost. I wanted to help him and I did. I helped build his career."

Clarice shrugged. "A few contacts."

"Major contacts," she snapped, her gaze turning to stone. "Can't you see when you're being used? You've done so much for him, but he'll get tired of you one day. There will always be younger women. Richer women."

"Please don't—"

"He's been saddled with his nephew, who's absolutely adorable by the way. I can see why you feel for him—"

"Mom—"

"He just sees you as a mother figure."

"That's not true."

"How do you know? How do you know what his true motives are?"

"I know."

"You don't."

"Yes, I do."

"Then prove it. I'll go see Faiza's baby, if you stop see-ing him."

For a moment she couldn't breathe. She gripped the front of her jacket unable to believe such an ultimatum. "What?"

"You heard me."

"No. I. Didn't," Clarice said each word taking an effort to say.

"Either you—"

Clarice gathered the collar of her coat, tighter against the evening chill. "Why should I have to stop seeing someone I care about so that—"

"Because if you want me to suffer you should too. Don't you realize you're asking me to do the impossible?"

"I only thought—"

"You didn't think at all," Lois shot back. "If you're not willing to hurt then neither am I. I don't think you've ever really understood what your sister did to me."

"I do," Clarice said shocked. "I have. But if you want someone to blame it was Carl's fault too. He shouldn't have agreed to the wedding."

"He loved me! *She* changed his mind."

"Mom."

"If you really believe Drew loves you then you have nothing to worry about."

"You're talking about two different things."

"No, I'm not. How much do you love this man? How much are you willing to risk? Are you hesitating because you know that he might leave you one day and you'll have no one to turn to?"

That had been a private fear, but she knew Drew wasn't like Carl. He wouldn't do what he didn't want to. He was true. "I'm not giving him up."

Lois got into her car then shot her daughter a venomous glance, which came and went so quickly Clarice wasn't sure she'd seen it at first. But she had and for the first time Clarice felt the sting of her mother's envy. She finally realized her mother didn't like to see her happy and whose happiness was what she had to choose—her mother's, her sister's or her own.

Chapter Thirty

"Was the lemon cake a hit?" Drew asked the moment Clarice returned to the apartment.

Clarice closed the door behind her. "Where's Theo?"

"In his bedroom. What's wrong?"

"She doesn't want me to see you anymore." When he didn't respond she added, "She thinks that you're using me."

His expression darkened. "Is she still out there?" he asked, making a move for the door.

Clarice sat down on the couch. "No, she just left."

He stared at her stunned. "What did I do wrong? What has she got against me?"

"It's really not about you. It's about Faiza."

He sat down beside her. "Faiza? How does she fit in?"

Clarice briefly told him about Stone and Faiza's request. "If I break up with you then Mom says she'll see Faiza's son."

"Damn, and I thought *my* parents were scary."

"I know it's emotional blackmail and I know why she's doing it, but Faiza really needs her."

"What about me?" Drew asked in a too soft tone. "You?"

He nodded.

"You don't need me. Not the way——"

"Faiza needs you?" he finished in a sour tone. "Or your mother? Is it because I don't need you enough? Is that my crime? Maybe it was better when I had back spasms and a business that wasn't going anywhere. Would it be harder to give me up then?"

"No," Clarice said her voice cracking with pain. "It's not that. It's just I've been in this tug of war so long and I want it to end."

"It can end without you."

"How?"

"Just walk away. Live your life. Don't let them tell you what to do anymore. See your sister if you want to, talk to your mother, and see me. Do whatever you want."

"It's easy for you to say."

He stared at her for a long moment then said in a tense voice, "*Easy* for me?"

"Yes, you were able to do what you wanted not caring what your parents thought when you gave up your scholarship, when you took over Delites, when you stepped in to raise Theo. You live by your own rules."

"I did what I had to."

"I know. My sister said the same when she ran off with Carl. But I can't do that. I can't hurt others just so that I can live my life. I see the wreckage left. I can't turn away from that."

"Nothing has been easy about the choices I've made. It's been hard, sometimes lonely, sometimes painful, but I knew I had to live my life on my terms."

"I'm not saying you didn't work hard," Clarice said, softening her tone, hoping he'd understand. "I'm just saying that I'm not you. That I can't have the same cavalier attitude that you and Faiza have."

His tone hardened. "Don't compare me to your sister."

"You both don't care what other people think." She tapped her chest. "I do. Maybe too much, but I do."

He sighed then stood. "Fine, then you'd better go before Theo sees you."

She stared up at him, helpless. "Drew. I haven't made up my mind yet."

"Yes, you have. You're just too afraid to say it."

She stood and faced him. "That's not true. I'm just thinking aloud. The last time, after meeting your parents, you said that it was all right if I told you how I felt."

"I was wrong. I don't want to hear it. I don't want to hear you defending your sister any more or your mother. I don't want to feel like I constantly might lose you. You're right, we're not the same. You know how I feel. You never have to doubt me, but with you..." He shook his head. "I don't know whether you'll lie to me or hold me close."

"When have I lied to you?"

"You don't do it with words. It's what you don't say." He rested his hands on his hips. "It doesn't matter now."

"So you're making the choice for me?"

Drew closed his eyes and hung his head. "Just go," he said, holding himself still, afraid she might speak or touch him and shatter his resolve.

"You didn't give me a chance all those years ago either. When you asked me out you didn't give me a chance to reply. I should have known you hadn't changed."

Drew didn't move. He remained still until he heard the front door close.

She hated them all! Her mother, Drew, Faiza! All of them. Clarice drove home, fury filling her veins. How quickly they could toss her away. She, who had loved each and every one of them with all her heart, but she wouldn't anymore. She would live for herself. She would live life on her terms without them. She never wanted to see any of them again. Ever.

She'd start a new life. She'd give her notice at the accounting firm. Maybe she'd even put her townhouse up for sale then disappear where they couldn't find her.

Clarice laughed at the thought. Not that they would look for her. They would all go on with their lives. Faiza had her family, Drew had Theo (how she would miss Theo and Lady!) and he was young with a successful business, he'd have his choice of ladies. Her mother worried her most, but Clarice knew she would survive.

They all would. She'd fooled herself into believing she was the key to their survival when in truth they really didn't need her.

Clarice pulled her car to the side of the road, blinded by tears. She'd given up her life for nothing. Buried her dreams for people who didn't care. She'd been a fool and that was no one's fault but her own.

She rested her head on the steering wheel, sobs wracking her body. *I loved you, Drew. You bastard! I would have done anything for you. I thought I could share my feelings. I thought I could trust you. But I was wrong.*

She lifted her head and stared out at the headlights cutting through the dark evening. She wiped her eyes. It was time to depend on herself. To follow her heart and leave them all behind. She was free. Free from them all. Free to make her own choices. Free to not care who got hurt.

Clarice pulled out her cell phone, steadied her voice then said, "Hello Luisa? I need to talk to you."

Chapter Thirty-one

"You look like a man who could use a drink," Murray said, when he saw Drew, closing up.

Drew didn't realize how much he'd been holding his breath until he saw Murray's smiling face. He hadn't seen him for nearly three weeks. He'd wondered if something had happened to him. He needed something in his life to stay the same. "You buying?"

"Of course."

Moments later they sat in a quiet bar with two half empty glasses between them.

"I've got all night if you want to talk," Murray said.

Drew bit his lip then leaned back in his chair. "Are you a mind reader?"

"No. I just sense things and you look like a man who needs to get a few things off his chest."

"Hmm."

Murray sat back and pointed at him. "Let me guess. Women troubles?"

Drew took a long swallow then set his glass down. "That's an easy guess."

"Am I right?"

He nodded. "Unfortunately."

"Things aren't working out between you and your girlfriend?"

"It's not us," Drew said, frustration making his voice hard. "It's her family. I thought my family had issues, but hers…" Drew shook his head. "Her mother and sister are…I don't know."

"Do you think they're too much to handle?"

"No, if only she would see what they're doing."

"I say give up on her."

Drew's eyes flashed. "Why?"

Murray held up his hands in surrender. "I'm just offering some advice. Have you talked to her?"

Drew tapped his thumb against the glass and looked away.

"So you already gave up on her," Murray guessed. "Good for you."

Drew turned to him annoyed. "It's not like that. I didn't want to. I didn't have a choice."

Murray nodded. "I understand. You don't want a woman that's too tied to her family. She'll bring you all kinds of trouble."

"Is that why you got divorced? You had trouble with your wife's family?"

A smile touched his lips. "Something like that."

Drew shook his head. "I didn't want to give her up, but…"

"But what?"

"I had to do it before she gave me up first."

"How do you know she was going to give you up?"

Drew tapped the table. "She was given a choice and I just knew… I just knew by the way she was talking and the expression on her face."

"Which can speak louder than words."

"Right."

"Unless you're used to hiding your feelings."

Drew paused. "What?"

"Then it's hard for people to read you. You're so used to mirroring back to people what they want to see, that they stop seeing you anymore. They only see what they want to see. When Clarice told me about you, I'd hoped you would be different."

Drew paused with his glass halfway to his lips. "What?"

Murray held out his hand. "I suppose it's time I fully introduce myself. I'm Murray Yates. Clarice's father."

Drew set his glass down hard. "She told you about me?"

"Months ago. I'm one of the few people she can truly be herself with. We trust and understand each other. I didn't mean to come by as many times as I did, but your food is addictive." He smiled.

Drew didn't return the expression. "Were you spying on me?"

"Does it matter now?"

Drew finished his drink.

"My wife left me because I was too boring. I didn't realize it. I thought our nearly twenty years together had been the best part of my life. I'm saddened that our daughter hurt her the way she did, but Lois and Faiza have a lot more in common than they would ever admit."

"What are you trying to say?"

"That's the problem with you. You keep needing more words when you have proof staring you in the face."

"Proof?"

"I'm not sitting here because I have time on my hands. I'm sitting here because my daughter loves you. Do you think it was easy for her to tell me about you? I knew about you before you even thought of introducing her to your family. Before your business was booming. You have no idea how proud of you she was." Murray sighed. "The truth is it's better this way because you didn't just let her go, you let her down."

He hadn't let her down, Drew thought a few days later as he added cream cheese frosting to a pumpkin cake that he planned to put in the display case.

She should have told him about her father. She should have told him that she loved him. "Right, Stuart?" he mumbled. "It's not my fault."

But he still felt guilty. He hated how Murray made him feel as if he hadn't trusted her. As if he'd failed her somehow. The sad truth was he had. He'd been so afraid to lose her that he'd pushed her away. He sighed and whispered under his breath, "How do I get her back, Stuart?"

He finished the cake then stood back to inspect it when he felt a tap on his shoulder. "Where's your phone?" Penny asked.

"In my office. Why?"

"Your mother has been trying to reach you. She called the main line."

His heart started to race. She rarely called him at work. He disappeared into his office and called her. His mother's tear soaked voice told him all he need to know, he barely heard her words. He felt his mouth move but didn't know what he said before he hung up.

He'd been expecting the call, known it would come, but it still gutted him. His throat closed so he couldn't speak. He nodded instead. He wouldn't cry, although he could feel tears stinging behind his eyes; he wouldn't think of Theo, he'd get to that later; he wouldn't call Clarice although every part of his being screamed for him to do so.

He'd handle this on his own.

Don't! another voice said, a familiar voice he'd longed to hear. *Go to her. If not for you, for Theo. Tell her how you feel.*

Chapter Thirty-two

The pounding on her front door surprised her. Clarice looked through the peephole then swung open the door. "Drew, what—"

"You weren't at your office," he said barreling into the room.

"No," Clarice said, cautiously closing the door unable to read his mood. "I only work there part-time now."

He nodded and rubbed his chin.

"Do you want to sit down?"

He shook his head. "I came to tell you that I was wrong. I'm sorry I told you to leave. I didn't mean it." He rested his hands on his hips and took a deep breath. "And I'll give it up. I'll focus on business instead of baking. I'll open another shop and bring in more money so that you can quit and work fulltime at what you love."

Clarice lightly touched his arm. And for a moment she saw herself at twenty-six when she'd given up her dreams, when she'd stopped her life because of someone she loved and she realized that if her mother had loved her back, she wouldn't have needed Clarice to sacrifice a thing. "Drew, slow down. You don't know what you're saying."

His eyes darkened with emotion. "I'm saying that I love you. That I don't want to lose you. That I'll do whatever it takes to—"

"Drew—"

"No, let me finish. I was a coward and I hurt you. Give me another chance. I'll help you with Faiza and your mother so—"

"No."

He paused. "Sorry?"

"I said 'no.' I don't need you to do that. They both won't talk to me."

"They'll come around and—"

"I don't care anymore," she said, although it wasn't completely true. It still hurt her that Faiza was upset that Clarice wouldn't follow her mother's demands 'even for a moment' so that she would see Stone. She remembered their conversation a couple weeks ago.

"Carl told me about the surgery," Clarice had told her. "He said that Stone will be alright."

"But anything could happen and you should—"

"I've done all that I could for you. It's time you two deal with this on your own. I'm living my life now."

A part of her had thought her sister would be happy for her, that she would applaud her for having the courage she'd told her she'd lacked, but her sister had surprised her with her bitterness.

And that was when Clarice realized that Faiza had assuaged her guilt in Clarice's servitude. As long as Clarice was unhappy, her sister felt free to be happy. But once Clarice threw away that burden, Faiza had to face the choice she'd made. She had to see that as happy as her life was there would always be a price to pay for what she and Carl had done.

Her mother also had to face the fact that Clarice's misery hadn't eased her own. That she'd chosen to give up eight years, and acknowledge that the pain she'd stayed with was the prison she'd chosen and she no longer had someone to share it with.

Clarice still loved them both and hoped that they would one day realize that she wouldn't choose between them, but she would no longer put her life on hold until they figured that out.

"I don't need your help with my family," Clarice told him.

Drew ducked his head in the familiar way that made him look both fierce and vulnerable but this time he also looked more miserable than she'd ever seen him. "Then tell me what to do to win you back. I lost Stuart, he passed away today and I can't lose you too. I need you. Please."

Clarice wrapped her arms around him and held him close, her heart aching for him. "I'd already chosen you. I didn't plan on letting you go."

Drew squeezed his eyes shut and buried his face in her neck, relief mingling with anguish. "I missed you so much and now…" He let the words fade away unable to finish.

"Does Theo know yet? About his father?"

Drew shook his head. "I can't believe how much it hurts," he said. "Even though I knew it would happen."

"Do you want me to be with you when you tell him?"

He hesitated then nodded, allowing her to take his hand.

Lois sat alone at her dining room table, semi-dazed, wondering how her life had gotten to this point. She finished a glass of red wine and poured herself another as she glanced at her empty plate. Her dinner hadn't filled her, she wasn't sure anything would anymore. How had she managed to lose so much when all she'd wanted was a life of more excitement, more adventure, more love?

She paused with the glass to her lips when she heard the doorbell. Her heart lifted. Could it be Clarice? "Coming," she said then opened the door and saw her ex-husband.

"What are you doing here?" she said more out of curiosity than anger.

Murray walked passed her with the same slow gait that used to bother her, now it gave her a sense of calm, as did his quiet voice. "Would you like to go for coffee?"

Relief gripped her; she wouldn't have to face her loneliness tonight. She wouldn't have to wallow in regrets; she could push them aside for awhile and be with someone who accepted her flaws. "Yes, coffee sounds wonderful."

Theo dreamed of his father dancing with the angels on clouds that tasted like candy floss and stars as sweet as sugar.

He cried sometimes because he still missed him, but he was happy that his uncle and grandparents weren't as angry as before and he didn't have to worry about his grandparents trying to take him.

He looked out his new bedroom window at the budding sugar maple in the backyard, a sign that spring was finally here, Lady sitting by his side wagging her tail, while the scent of cinnamon rolls wafted through the air from the kitchen.

"Theo!" his uncle called.

He raced to the kitchen, still surprised how much more room Clarice's townhouse had, and found his uncle and Clarice icing the rolls at the counter. "Yes?"

Drew handed him a spatula. "Help her. She's terrible at this."

"I am not," Clarice said, slowing smoothing the icing.

Drew shook his head, watching more icing landing on the tray than the roll. "You should stick with massage."

She shot him a glance. "That's the last time I help you when you get a leg cramp."

Theo pulled up a step stool. She was making a mess and he wanted to help her. "Let me show you, Aunty." He looked at his uncle. "Now I get to call her Aunty Clarice, right?" he asked since he'd still only been calling her Clarice.

Drew looked at Clarice and their eyes met. And for a moment Clarice was a bride once again, smiling as she stood beside a three-tiered ivory wedding cake decorated with purple grapes and small red flowers, the man she adored standing next to her. For Drew, his mind didn't go to the wedding ceremony or the cake, but the first time he came home to see Clarice helping Theo with his homework, his love for them both filling his heart.

He held his wife's gaze then grinned at his nephew and said, "Yes."

About the Author

Dara Girard is an award-winning, national bestselling author of more than thirty books including *Midnight Promise, Unexpected Pleasure, Just One Look* and *The Amber Stone*. Dara loves to travel and hear from readers.

You can write her at:
contactdara@daragirard.com
or
P.O. Box 10345
Silver Spring, MD 20914

If you'd like to receive a reply, please send a self-addressed stamped envelope. Visit daragirard.com to join her newsletter and be the first to find out about current and upcoming releases.

9 781949 764062